Hero Society

Fall

Jessica Florence

This is a work of fiction. Names, places, characters, and events are fictitious in every regard. Any similarities to actual events, and persons, living or dead, are purely coincidental. Any trademarks, service marks, product names, or named features are assumed to be the property of their respective owners and are used only for reference. There is no implied endorsement if any of those terms are used. Except for review purposes, the reproduction of this book in whole or part, electronically or mechanically, constitutes a copyright violation.

Jessica Florence© **2020**

Editing by Magnifico Manuscripts

Proofreading by Virginia Tesi Carey

Cover by Sarah Hansen, Okay Creations©

*This book contains sensitive material such as depression, suicide, and cutting. *

Prologue
2008
Selene

I wanted to die.

On the outside, I seemed like your normal angst-ridden eighteen-year-old, but on the inside, my soul screamed to end everything.

Death called to me like a siren's song. It rolled inside my veins, its very presence haunting my mind.

Although surrounded by many at the party, I felt so alone. People cared about me; people loved me. I hadn't come from horrid upbringings or even had life-altering occurrences that drove me to desire suicide.

No, this need was deeper.

"Selene! There you are, baby."

My boyfriend, Travis, came over to me with a beer in his hands. My body cringed at the scent. I hated alcohol and parties. But Travis thought it would be good for me to get out of my dark bedroom and be around people. He claimed I was gloomy all the time. I tried not to be, but gloom was inside my genetics.

"I wanna go home." My voice could barely be heard over the music blaring in this house.

Travis's pretty-boy face looked at me, and he shook his head, his blond hair sticking to his sweaty forehead with the movement.

"Let's just go somewhere quieter. Help clear your head." He set the beer down on a random table and wrapped his hands around mine sweetly. His touch was soothing, but I knew it wouldn't last long. Even now the call to find death was growing stronger, a constant battle in my head.

Travis had been kind to me, always a bright light during my darkest days. I liked that about him the most. He believed he could fight back whatever cloud hovered over me with his bright smile and funny charm. He led us past couples taking exhibitionism to a new level. Thankfully Travis hadn't pushed me to do anything like that in the three months we'd been dating.

"In here should be calmer. You can barely hear the music." He opened a door to a bedroom. My hand squeezed his nervously, my head running wild with the thought of being in a room like this with him. My eyes closed with anxiety, tensing my muscles one by one.

"Easy, Selene, it's OK, baby. I won't hurt you." His warm hands cupped my cheeks. I focused on my heartbeats, counting them, feeling my breath fill my chest, then contract.

"I'm OK." My eyes opened to look into his pretty blues. I wasn't OK, but I could fake it. When you hit your lowest, faking was all you could do to function. Pretend, pretend, pretend.

His hands dropped, believing my mask of contentment before walking over to the bed. I followed and sat gingerly on the quilted comforter. The room was lit by one single lamp on the nightstand and appeared bare, like an estranged spare bedroom.

"You're really pretty tonight. Did I tell you that already?" He leaned in a little closer, his lips pressing a kiss to my pointed nose.

"You did. You look handsome, too." He did. I tried to compliment him when I could. It helped show I cared to think about something other than the turmoil inside my head. His fingers inched up my sweater, feeling my arm beneath the soft material. A strange tingle shot up my arm, making my head quiet for a moment . . . no thoughts of death, no screaming inside me.

"Touch me," I whispered. His touch made me feel quiet and normal for a few seconds. It hadn't been like this before, but something was different now. Ever since I'd turned sixteen, everything had changed. Fighting it had been my only option. I tried to be the girl I was before—the sweet cheerleader with hopes of being a nurse, marrying well, and popping out kids to play behind the white picket fence. But challenging the darkness only made it worse.

"I'd love to." Travis answered my whisper and began touching me more. At first it was up my arms, then his lips were at my jaw, then my neck. He was drunk, and his movements were sloppy. But the tingle ran wild throughout me. It wasn't arousal. This was something different. I felt his hands. I felt the wetness and heat from his lips on my cool skin. Something about this was affecting my shade.

His hands moved up my shirt, gripping me harshly. I bit into my lip to stop from crying out. His other hand moved to my jeans, hastily trying to unclasp the button. I wanted the relief from the madness inside me, but I wasn't ready for this.

"Not this, Travis." I tried pushing him back.

"I won't hurt you, Selene. I promise, baby."

I believed him, but I still wasn't ready. My hands pushed harder against his chest as he leaned back to focus more on my jeans. His eyes widened as he lost his balance on the edge of the bed. The force from my push and his own body weight propelled him against the nightstand with a crash.

"Oh God, Travis, are you OK?" Instantly, I was at his side. Death permeated the air. The feeling settled over me like a warm blanket. The thrashing in my head was gone, and the tingle in my blood ran rampant.

"No, no, no."

My shaking hands touched his face, checking his features for signs of life. Blood soaked into the carpet beneath his head and coated the furniture. He'd hit the corner of the wood, proof of the injury he'd suffered.

"Selene?" His voice was clear, but his lips hadn't moved. His eyes were still closed, and there was no movement from his contracting and expanding chest.

"Selene?" I turned, hearing the voice behind me.

My blood-covered fingers went to my mouth to cover my gasp, the tang of copper slipping past my lips. He was there, shimmering like a ghost. "You're dead!" I cried against my hand, trying not to be too loud but also not believing what I was seeing. I'd seen people like this since turning sixteen, but I thought it was all in my head . . . the madness driving me every day toward a mental hospital.

Only there he floated like a ghost and not a trick of the brain. This was real.

"You have to take me on, Selene."

I shook my head, wanting no part of this.

"It's your job. Death calls to you, and you are Death."

Death was calling to me. The feeling was so strong that I wanted to join him, to feel the coldness start in my fingers, then move across my skin, consuming my mind . . . the sweet surrender to the darkness.

"No, baby. Not your time." He shook his iridescent head but I panicked. I needed a way out. This was too much for me to live with. I reached into Travis's pocket that I knew housed a small knife. No more faking I was OK. No more trying to smile when all I wanted to do was waste away. No more separation of soul and mind. I was going to become one in death.

The pain was nothing. Blood pooled into the carpet, and soon I would be free. Death called to me like a siren's song, a final kiss of darkness, and I was allured to its depths forever.

Chapter One
Present Day
Selene

"I don't wanna be here," I grumbled to my animated friend Emily, who could not sit still at the sight before her.

"You just wait and see. That story you've been dying to write for the paper is here." Her eyes never left the circular circus stage before us. Emily was a five-foot-seven ball of energy, with pink hair and freckles on top of her nose. Her smile was my favorite part of her physic. Emily's smile could instantly make you feel better about life, like a cup of hot chocolate with whipped cream on top.

She'd used that cozy grin on me many times after the incident with Travis's pocketknife. I'd killed myself in my insanity, but it wasn't my time to go. Doctors fixed me up, pumped me full of blood, and put me on twenty-four-hour suicide watch. After that my parents had me committed until I was better. Emily was one of the nurses who took care of me. She made sure I ate food and kept me company. The worst place someone who has mental issues can be is in their own head. Over the few months of being in the psych ward, we'd become friends, bonding over the desire of death but grew strong enough to resist.

Emily had been a cutter growing up. Thankfully I hadn't found an interest in that act. She had worked through her issues and wanted to help others. She didn't have any friends because she was too much for people to understand . . . like me.

Sometimes my long dirty-blond waves looked nice, like I put effort into my appearance. My normal black eyeliner was on point. Then there were times where I looked like I'd slept under a bridge. Mental health was no joke, and in reality, everyone battles some form of insanity. I've found the best thing you can do while feeling like you're stuck in the mud is make mud angels.

This week was a good week. Hell, I've actually been having a good few weeks. My desire to flirt with death was manageable, thanks to the Hero Society. After they'd come out to the world, explaining that people with powers came from the ancient Greek gods and goddesses, who in their final breaths cast their powers into the genes of mankind, hoping the powers would protect us mere humans. The powers came to the host the genes deemed worthy of them on a person's sixteenth birthday. If a person didn't use the powers, he or she would go mad.

Like me.

A man named Phillip Griffin and his friend Draco came to my home a year ago on a business visit. They were the leaders of the Hero Society. Draco had been immortal until he helped two others from the society change time for the better of mankind and their crew. His immortality was a price he paid gladly for saving his woman and the world. He'd known every power that could come forth in the human genes of the gods.

I thought I had been going crazy for years. Turns out my power made me a reaper. I couldn't kill someone like most would assume but I could feel when death was coming for someone's life. Once they died, I was to take their soul on. Of course, I found out there was an afterlife for us once we die. It had been working without me bringing souls up or down. I just happened to have the gift, and if I was around the soul, then I would take it where it was supposed to go. If I wasn't around there were other spirits that did the job. So while I wasn't needed per se, I still helped.

Since I was able to speak to those who recently passed, as well as a journalist who wanted the truth in everything, I helped settle unresolved cases with the Seahill Police Department. It was either use my gifts for the greater good or slip into madness again. I'd chosen to be a superhero and use those powers to help those who couldn't help themselves.

Most of the time the dead wanted to move on, but there were a few that refused. I'd try to help them so that they could move on peacefully. Forcing them to leave never worked in my favor. They tended to avoid me and disappear before I could grab them.

"Oh, it's about to start!" Emily's hands shook my arm, bringing me back to the present.

The lights dimmed on the plain black stage, signaling something was about to happen. Her fingers reached over and intertwined with mine. Sound started through hidden speakers all around us.

"Caw!" A screeching black crow flew past my head. My hair whirled from the bird's movement to the stage. A man appeared as if out of thin air, and the crow landed on his shoulder.

"That's him!" Emily whispered, squeezing my hand tighter.

What was it about this guy that intrigued her so? His head was tilted down, and an old top hat sat on his head. Fog crept onto the circle-like stage in front of us. My skin tingled and I hoped someone wasn't about to die on stage.

"As reality slips from your mind, your eyes widen with wonder, and your soul leaps onto the wind of a dream."

That voice. My spine straightened, and I stared at the man dressed in black with a ringleader's red coat. The timbre in his words demanded attention without yelling. A stomping sound shuddered throughout the small arena, just as his head popped up, and he looked into the crowd. At me.

"Prepare for the mystical."

His mouth didn't move, but the words came out like he'd said them. Then the crow on his shoulder laughed in the man's voice. That's not scary or anything. A talking crow being creepy on a mystery man's shoulders.

The lights came on and there were suddenly performers everywhere! Trapeze artists flew above, leaping into each other's hands, swinging back and forth. A woman on a tightrope jumped and danced along the thin wire. A smaller elephant with a small boy sitting on top of the elephant's back, lifted its body up onto a ball and walked around slowly. It was a spectacular show of all the various arts in performing. But there seemed to be something different about this circus than others I'd seen in the past.

Every player on the stage had an iridescent glow to them that did not come from the lights. The shimmer made their skin, hair, and clothes glow. The ringleader moved around the stage, working magic and orchestrating the acts in perfect synchronization.

An eerie feeling enveloped me as I realized I'd seen that glow before.

"Do they always shine like that?" I whispered to my enraptured friend's ear.

"Always. They are so shiny, they almost look like ghosts."

Then it hit me. This was no ordinary circus. Emily was right even though she didn't know it.

This was a circus filled with ghosts. But how?

Chapter Two
Selene

    I watched the ringmaster as he moved about the stage. He watched each performer doing their job at the right moment timed with the music. Somehow, he could see them or maybe even control the circus ghosts. I was so confused about what was happening that the more I tried to figure it out, the more I was lost.

    "It's so magical." Emily sighed in awe beside me.

    It was. If I wasn't so blind to the notion there were ghosts on the circular stage and everyone saw them, I would have had parted lips and a slack jaw like she did.

    The ringleader's presence demanded everyone's complete attention. Every move he made was precise; every impossibility he created was pure magic. The acts around him were magnificent and perfectly executed, like they'd been doing this for many more years than I'd been alive.

    So many questions.

    The tingle in my skin increased; pin and needle-like feeling pricked all over my body. Death was near. Was it the ghosts that gave me this sensation? They were dead, and this was not an uncommon feeling around the dead.

An ear-piercing scream echoed throughout the room. The horrifying noise was not part of the show. The ringleader ceased movement, his eyes on the crowd to my left. More people from that area began to scream, shouting for help.

"I'll be back!" I yelled at Emily, the room becoming louder in the panic. Through the crowd of hysterical people, I waded toward where the screaming had started. A shimmer—two shimmering forms could be seen, but then the crowd got in my way as it tried to get away from the dead. One of the deceased had vanished, moving on to the afterlife with a collector spirit like myself or had been a spectator.

A woman stood above a dead body, an exact mirror in looks. She was confused, as many are when they gaze upon their former body. No one else could see her . . . just me. Everyone else who stayed near us were either crying or calling 911. One person applied pressure with her sweater on the blood oozing out of the woman who was already gone.

"I don't understand." Her voice was soft, barely above a whisper. Her gaze lifted up, finding mine on her.

"Do you know what happened?" I probed, and she shook her head.

"I had just come back from . . ." She paused, her face scrunching up as she thought hard about where she was or what she had been doing. It happened a lot—the memory loss after death. People were already so distraught and confused that they tended to forget their last moments unless it was important. Wherever she had been wasn't important, and I doubt she knew the identity of her killer.

"Is that me?" Her shimmering face looked down at the bleeding body, while her hand went to her mouth in shock.

"I'm sorry." I offered my condolences, but there wasn't anything I could do to fix it. I could only take her onward. My body hummed since I was so close to her. The feeling calmed me and gave me peace like it always did.

"Are you death?" She looked up at me and I shook my head.

"I'm not death, but I am a reaper. I'll take you on to where you are supposed to be, where you can be at peace." I smiled and reached my hand outward. I wasn't going to get much information from her in this confusion, and I'd already been drawing too much attention to myself standing by the body talking to what everyone else assumed was the wall instead of a ghost.

"I'm not ready to be dead." She pursed her lips and looked back down at her body, already turning pale from the blood draining onto the red carpet.

"You can choose to stay but you will become a lost soul, and trust me, you don't want that. Moving on is where you belong. It'll be OK. You will be OK, and everyone you love will be happier with the thought that you've found peace in death."

Her hand raised toward mine. I felt my body lightening, like I was becoming one with the air, feeling that nothing else in the world could touch me and I was as close to heaven as I could get.

"What's your name?" I asked, as her shaking hand clasped onto mine.

"Lindsey Walters."

I closed my eyes, feeling the warmth and light of where Lindsey was needed. I didn't know exactly if heaven or hell were truly real. I just knew that when I held onto a soul, I felt myself being drawn to places of eerie quietness or peace.

It was like an out of body experience. I was able to travel in both realms of the living and the dead . . . seer of both. Normal humans never saw what I was doing. I was aware of people around me but couldn't talk. I was in two places at once when I assisted souls onward.

Lindsey slowly disappeared into the warm light, and I knew she found peace. Instantly I was back in my own head and took a few steps backward to move away from the scene as paramedics arrived. Chaos erupted, and cops swarmed the place.

My focus darted around and suddenly became vulnerable by a pair of piercing blue eyes. The ringleader stared like he saw me as I was, reaper, and he was not afraid.

A shimmering blue hand from the female trapeze ghost rested on his shoulder and she murmured something in his ear, then nodded toward the edge of the stage. I couldn't tear my gaze away from him; the connection I felt toward death was with him, like a tether pulling us closer, weaving our destinies together into a morbid tapestry.

I always battled with fate . . . that my life was planned and I had no choice. Sometimes I felt this was true, and sometimes I believed I was the captain of my own ship . . . that I created my own destiny.

But in those eyes, those blue knowing eyes, I felt a stir in the cosmos, with an unrelenting feeling of fate solidifying my course.

"Miss, I need you to back up, please." A police officer cut me off from the ringleader on the stage, and I felt like I could breathe again.

"Of course, so sorry." It was my time to go. Emily was waiting for me where we had been sitting, and I walked over to join her.

"You OK?" I asked, noticing she was pale and shaken up.

"Yeah, I just feel bad, and kinda makes you think of your own mortality, ya know? Could be one of us."

That was something I did understand . . . how death didn't discriminate. Rich, poor, young, or old . . . death came no matter what and could happen at any time. I wrapped my arms around her, then we began walking toward the exit. As if I couldn't help myself, I turned to look at the stage one last time to see him staring at me still. The intensity of his stare should have scared me, but I wasn't afraid.
I turned away, and we walked into the lobby to give our statements as a witness to the scream.

Chapter Three

Jude

"What the fuck happened?" I slammed the newspaper down on my dining table and slumped into the chair beside it. I was fucked. My whole show was fucked.

"The police are working on it. There isn't anything else you can do." Lucille's hand touched my shoulder and I shrugged it off. I knew what she wanted from me, but it wasn't happening. I was never comfortable with her history of having an affair with my grandfather and then my dad.

"I could go ask her what happened." It was an option.

"I think you should just focus on living out the next month the way you wanted to, which was doing your show."

She's right, and I fucking hate it. All part of the curse that shattered my family. The gates to the realm of the dead must stay closed, and the way to keep them sealed is with the blood of a Mallory man. Fortunately, all we seemed to have in our family were boys, so lucky curse.

All children in my family were born on Halloween, had to pay the debt on their thirtieth birthday. I was going to have to die on my birthday in thirty days. While my dad, grandfather, and great-grandfather chose to get married and have kids, I decided I didn't want to have that life only to leave it. I avoided contact with people who I could see myself getting close to. Sure, I got lonely, and during desperate times I would find company with a cold-as-ice woman who had no heart.

It sucked, but it was either that or fall in love and have to choose between saving the world from the dead rising or my family. Easiest choice was to live out my life and then die, ending this curse with me.

"Yeah, you're right." I closed my eyes and rested my head against the tall back of the chair. It was selfish, and I hated it. This whole mess wasn't fair, but it couldn't be changed.

"If you need anything . . ." She let the rest of her sentence drift off just before I felt her cold lips press against my cheek. Her heels clicked along the old wood floors, and I deflated internally hearing her disappear into the hall outside.

"She really needs to get a life. You're not going to sleep with her." My body tensed up for a second before relaxing and opening my eyes to see my friend.

"She's just trying to make it down the family tree before you all go on." I shrugged, and Rudy grinned while sitting on the chandelier in a ghost-like form. There wasn't anything left in this world to surprise me after living in a house filled with ghosts all my life. Most of them left me alone; we'd gotten used to each other years ago.

"Any news about the girl from the show?" With the expertise of an acrobat, Rudy leapt off the chandelier and landed on the table. It didn't move or shudder under the weight because ghosts weren't in real form. My power only made them mostly human for a time being. All part of the deal we made. They give me a hell of a show, and I take them with me into the afterlife.

"No, the police have identified her, and I recognize her as one of the fans that had come backstage with VIP access, but nothing else." I sat up and clasped onto the newspaper, hoping to catch something in the words that I didn't already know.

"And the other girl?"

Rudy was one of the only people I would consider a friend . . . my best friend. Had I been alive before he died, we probably would have caused trouble all over the place. We would have looked alike, too—same Mediterranean-tan skin, blue eyes, and dark-brown hair. Now he was a light blue unless I used my power over the dead to change it.

Since he was my best friend, he was the only person I told about the woman in the audience whose soul sang to mine. She saw the dead girl, and it looked like she knew my crew were not human performers. I'd yet to know someone who had a gift like mine. Whoever she was, she intrigued me, and that was not a good thing.

"No."

"Too bad, she was hot. In a sort of combat boots, grunge kind of way. Bet she'd be way more fun in the sack than Lucy."

I rolled my eyes. Lucy was a serious pain in my ass. Even with a month left to live, I wasn't going to give in to use my powers just for sex like everyone else in my family was prone to doing. It was the only chance she could feel real again, so she used it to her advantage. I couldn't blame her, though. If I was dead, couldn't feel warmth, or taste anything, I'd do whatever it took to gain some sensation in my immortal life.

"Neither will be happening. I've only got a month left. Not going to spend it with a woman." Rudy knew how I felt. I wanted to put on the show of a lifetime then disappear.

"Yeah, yeah. I get it. Still, you only live once, right? It's what the kids these days say. YOLO." Using a bit of my power gifted from Hades, I pushed the poor fool off the table in a brotherly manner.

"We're going to have to have a fair fight before we go, you and me." He stood off the ground and started throwing punches that felt like a light breeze against my cheek.

"I'll let you get a good one in soon. I promise. YOLO, right?" I wanted this cursed life to end already. I was ready for the peace the other side would bring. No more curses or responsibility of keeping the dead in their place or ghosts trying to sleep with me. One month to go.

There wasn't anything I could do about the dead girl from the show or the mystery woman right now so I stood and pulled on the invisible tethers tying me to the souls under my control. There were times I was grateful that this antebellum-style mansion, as creepy as it was, I called home. Plenty of space to practice circus acts in the ballroom.

"Let's go rehearse for the show."

Chapter Four
Selene

"Call me as soon as you get home! I want to hear every single detail!"

For a moment I thought Emily was going to crawl out of my phone so she could be here in person, but that was not a power she possessed.

"I promised I would. I'm almost there."

At least, I hoped I would. The address I'd found for one Jude Mallory had to have been a mistake because I was in the middle of nowhere.

"Eek, I can't wait. OK, I'll let you go. Take care." Her voice turned to a whisper and I guessed her boss was nearby at work. Glad I didn't have that problem. I tossed my phone in the passenger seat of my sedan without taking my focus off the winding road outside of Seahill.

"In one hundred feet, your destination will be on the right," the GPS announced but I still didn't see it. Nothing but trees and fog, which only added an eerie vibe to this whole mission. No one besides the police had been able to talk to the ringleader of *Mystical* about the death that happened at his show. We'd ran a story about the incident in the paper, but the big bosses wanted to know more about the mysterious man and his circus of ghosts. Of course, they didn't know it was a ghost circus like I did, but that had me volunteering to be the one to get a story. Hopefully I would be able to help solve the murder of Lindsey while I was at it.

It had been two days since she died, and none of the detectives on the case could figure out what happened besides she was stabbed, then bled to death. I had seen the shimmer of another soul near Lindsey's as I approached. Someone else had been there then disappeared just before I could see them. There was only one other person who could see them.

"Your destination is on the right."

"Shit." I slammed on my brakes and looked to the right for the driveway. I hadn't been paying attention and almost missed it. Once my heart was calm and my breathing back to its normal rhythm, I scanned the two-car-wide driveway that seemed to grow out of the woods. I would have driven right by it if I didn't have the GPS telling me I was here.

For a man who had many successes in his career of magic, I was surprised by the gates sealing the entrance to what appeared to be a long driveway covered in vines. It looked like no one had lived here in ages . . . centuries maybe.

"This can't be right." I looked at the address and then at the gate again.

Pulling my car off to the side of the road, I got out and threw the small journalist backpack I had over my shoulders. The weather was gloomy, and it started sprinkling rain as I walked toward the gate. The vibe combination of the weather and the deserted driveway was fit for a man who had a circus full of ghosts.

Technically hopping over the brick wall was trespassing, but if no one was here to report it, then it didn't matter. From my first observation, I assumed there would be a deserted house instead of a rich ringleader at the end of the driveway.

It took three minutes of walking over countless dead leaves beneath my feet until the trees cleared and I saw it. An algae-covered pond rested before a giant mansion with four large columns at its front. It looked like something you would see in Louisiana and not the Pacific Northwest of the country. It had a wraparound porch, multiple fireplace stacks, a small rounded tower in the middle, and a large atrium. Not something you see every day here. I felt like my feet were stuck on the cobblestone driveway in awe of this magnificent piece of architecture. Someone put a lot of effort and care into designing this mansion. I dug out my camera and snapped a shot for myself. Even if this house turned out to be nothing for the story I needed, I wanted to look at this place again. It would forever haunt my dreams with the dark spruce pines and dead leaves from the forest blowing against the immense structure.

There appeared to be no lights on inside the house as far as I could tell, and no one had come out to tell me to scram yet, either. As I walked closer, the tingle in my blood began to grow. Death was near . . . somewhere. I scanned the landscape, searching for shimmering blue souls, but I found none . . . yet.

I walked up wooden steps to the house, observing the intricate details carved into the double doors. This house was a work of art, and I couldn't stop staring at it.

After three knocks on the door, I waited patiently to see if someone was here. Hopefully it would be Mr. Mallory and he wouldn't be pissed that I hopped his wall to get here, but sometimes in journalism you had to do somethings that weren't always on the good side. Impatiently, I knocked two more times and yelled "hello" with no reply. I peeked in through the windows near the door just in case someone was a slow walker.

The thick curtains didn't give me much wiggle room to see inside the dusty windows but I could tell whoever was in there did not have a housekeeper. It looked as old and deserted as the outside did. A solid foundation and good building skills were all I could give credit to this house for still standing.

"Just a little peek around the back won't hurt anyone," I whispered to myself, looking back at the door which remained closed and began walking quietly around the corner of the house. The atrium was gorgeous, and I saw various plants and sculptures inside. Live plants, despite the cover of the metal and glass, kept the misty rain from falling on their leaves. I hopped off the porch and walked around the atrium, looking through the once-again dirty glass and saw a library beyond the assortment of plant life. Nobody dead or human walked in the library now.

I tilted my head, listening for anyone opening a door. Surely it would creak or be loud as fuck, since it was made of heavy, solid wood. Still nothing, so I kept walking and observing the layout of the house.

"Holy shit!" I was surprised the words came out of my mouth instead of my breath staying stuck inside my lungs. I thought the house was the surprise in these woods with its glorious appeal, but I should have guessed there would be another mystery.

A cemetery.

A cemetery so vast with mausoleums, tombs, and headstones everywhere. I'd never seen anything like it except in pictures of New Orleans cemeteries. The owner of the house must have been from New Orleans to have put so much of its culture just outside of Seahill. My hands went to my mouth in disbelief at the many ghosts lingering by limestone and marble tombstones of the graveyard.

A joyous voice from behind me laughed and then two hands pushed me with enough force that I couldn't keep my footing and began rolling down the hill into an endless gathering of the dead.

Chapter Five
Selene

"Ah!" I cried out as my body slammed into a headstone. The marble held like it had since 1873.

As if my entrance into the cemetery was a green light, all the souls began to come out from wherever they hid. Music and laughter filled the air as people had their fun with their eternal damnation on Earth.

"Take that, you pirate!" A ghost with a sword and an old British wig lunged with his sword at a . . . well . . . a pirate.

I'd never seen souls this old. Everyone in Seahill had been newly dead. These souls were centuries-old, different generations of souls having one hell of a party.

"Excuse me." I stood and rushed to a woman dressed in a Victorian-age outfit. Her ringlet curls bounced along her face as she turned to face me. When she noticed I wasn't a ghost, she gasped and floated away in another direction.

"What the hell is happening here?" I cursed as a rush of happiness flowed through me. Surrounded by so many souls, I had the itch to touch them, to bring them onward. It felt like the caress of a man against my neck. I wanted to lean into them and do as my own soul craved. I stumbled to crawl back up the hill I'd been pushed down but the ground was wet and my boots had trouble gripping the slick mud.

There had to be stairs and an entrance to this cemetery from the mansion. It was my only exit plan that had sense. If I stayed much longer, these ghosts were going to be deported and I wasn't sure that was a good thing, yet. There was a much greater mystery here and I needed the souls around to ferret out the truth. Who the hell pushed me? Ghosts did not have power like that, unless someone had given it the power.

"A fleshie!"

"She's alive."

Ghosts gasped in awe as I walked into the cemetery in the direction I'd hoped would bring me to the entrance.

"Might I be of some use, my lady? It's not very often we have such pretty guests in our lovely home." A balding man wearing fancy clothes and shiny shoes bowed before me like a gentleman. I didn't sense malice in his soul. If he were to move onward, he'd definitely see the lighter side of the afterlife.

"I need to get out of here." If a ghostly escort was all I was going to get, then I would take it.

"This way, my lady." He gestured straight ahead and lifted his arm up for me to rest mine atop. I didn't think it would work but I raised my arm to his. It fell through, of course.

"Sorry. Old habits," he apologized, his head bowing softly before looking me in the eyes and we began walking through the cemetery together.

"How are you guys still here?"

"How can you see us?" he countered before answering my question.

"I'm a reaper," I answered honestly and noticed he didn't move away from me, which took me by surprise. If they've been around long enough, they surely knew what I was and what I could do.

"You're not afraid?"

"No, no, dear lady. We are stuck here. Even if you tried, you couldn't take us onward despite how many wish you could." He gave me a sad smile and then looked at the souls who danced among the headstones.

What he said didn't make sense. None of this did.

"Be kind to my dearest great, great nephew. He didn't ask for this life, but it's the curse us male Mallorys face. He's a good boy." The kind soul attempted to pat me on the shoulder, then pointed toward our left. A grand staircase with large vases every ten feet led up to the large back veranda of the mansion.

"Thank you for helping me . . ." My words drifted off when all I saw was a tomb next to me. The soul had gone back into the cemetery. I looked at the cemetery and felt the euphoric sensation turn into a calming high. All of this was so strange.

I mentally cursed the stairs as I took the first step up. Exercise was not one of my favorite hobbies. I thought people who woke up every day and worked out because they enjoyed it were crazy. However, they were probably better off mentally and physically than I was, and happier, too. Unless something was after me, I was not a runner. These stairs would fill my exercise quota for the rest of the year.

By the time I made it to the veranda, I was tired, hungry, and a little pissy at myself and at Jude Mallory. I probably should have just reached out to him via his agent, or emailed, or written a letter. But he never did interviews, and I doubted he would have answered any of my inquiries. This was his fault. My irritated brain focused on that, as I walked up to the back door and gripped the handle like I owned the place.

"Mr. Mallory! Anybody home?" I yelled at the top of my lungs and waited by the opened doors.

Two souls dressed in circus attire came through the wall by the atrium and stared at me in shock.

"Rudy, that voice was really good. Nice trick." A tall, live man walked around the corner with a grin on his face, then stopped as he noticed me and realized the voice hadn't come from who he thought it did.

"Uh, who are you?" He ran his tan fingers through his dark brown hair and looked at his two ghost friends, then back at me.

"I'm Selene Constance from the *Seahill Sun Times*. I'm also working with the Seahill Police Department on the case of Lindsey Walters. I wanted to speak with you, ask a few questions. I knocked on the door but no one answered, so I thought this place was abandoned. It's very lovely, Mr. Mallory." He was still staring at me, not with anger in his expression but more of a stunned look, like he didn't know what to do with a live person in his house.

"It's Jude."

We stood there like idiots, watching each other. I had lost all thoughts and nothing mattered but his eyes, his face with his trimmed beard, and those lips that begged me for a taste. I didn't understand the intense pull toward his soul. Usually the only time I felt like this was if someone was about to die. Unless he was destined to die shortly, then the draw toward death didn't make sense. None of this did.

I needed more answers to the mystery that was Jude Mallory, the ringleader living in a haunted mansion.

Chapter Six

Jude

"Why don't we go sit in the parlor room?" I didn't even wait for her answer before I walked toward the parlor where we could sit and be more comfortable.

I should have told this woman to fuck off and leave my property. Should have, but didn't. What was wrong with me?

Interviews were not something I enjoyed. Everyone wanted to get too personal, get to know the real me. Real me was an asshole who preferred to hang out with the dead than the living. There was no use getting to know anyone if I was just going to die. Some fans of the show and my work cry when they heard the news, but they would move on unlike friends or family who would grieve for much longer.

Accepting this Selene into my home unsettled me to my core. The woman from the show that talked to the dead girl, here, in my home.

Maybe I was just curious.

"Interesting place you have here. Very intricate and well . . ."

"Dusty, yeah. I don't have the patience to clean everything. There's really no point, anyways," I answered for her, knowing what she was going to say. I'd once thought of making the ghosts clean the place up but they were already suffering. Cleaning seemed more like a punishment fit for hell.

"You said it, so can't say I was rude or anything." She continued looking around as we made it into the parlor. I gestured for her to sit, and I took a seat on the loveseat opposite of the one she descended onto. She was beautiful with dirty blond hair that looked streaked with melted honey in it. I knew her blue eyes could peer into my soul. She looked haunted in her own way, though, and it wasn't just being here in the house. She had a heavy burden and it weighed on her with every move she made, the way she had to force herself to sit tall and push confidence into her very being.

We sat there, neither one of us saying a word in this awkward situation. A few of my ghostly friends peeked in, unaware someone else in this room could see them.

"She is definitely a looker. Man, I thought she was hot back at the show. She is smoking now." Rudy came over to sit next to me, his mouth gaping at the woman before us, whose knowing smirk promised sweet revenge.

"Why, thank you, I didn't know if this sweater was complimentary to my body but I guess if I'm smokin then it must be great."

I laughed at the shock on Rudy's face. Serves the asshole right.

"You can see us? Holy shit, Jude. You're not the only one! Oh girl, I have been on the other side too long. I could use another flesh-and-blood person to live vicariously through." Rudy sat down next to her, filled with excitement.

"Rudy, give the woman some space." I watched her expression carefully to see if she was scared or annoyed at my friend, but she seemed content, like his presence relaxed her in some way.

"It's OK. But I wouldn't touch me if I were you. I'm a reaper, so taking dead people to the afterlife is my superpower." She shrugged, like having that sort of power was no big deal, but I knew differently. It was a power from Hades, the god of the underworld. The old gods had killed off their children, the demigods, and mankind lost faith in them. They were dying but still wanted to protect humans so they put their powers out into the world into the DNA of mortals. Lucky people were picked to host "said gifts" to help the world.

My gift was control over the dead, which sounded cool but it wasn't useful in stopping a bank robbery, unless the person got shot and we wanted information or I created an army of the dead to stop the criminals. Neither was really a good idea.

Ghosts on this plane of Earth couldn't do harm like they could in the movies. They couldn't shake doors or attack you. My family was the key to keeping it that way.

"They can't be sent onward by a reaper, even though I'm sure they would appreciate it." I figured I'd make everyone in the room feel more at ease with Selene around.

"The man out in the cemetery said something like that. Your great-great uncle, I believe."

She wasn't writing anything down, but Selene could be committing every detail to memory. I wasn't sure if being in a house filled with ghosts or having a cemetery had any relationship to the woman's death at my show.

"Phineas. That old man is a hoot." Rudy smiled at Selene, smitten as a ghost could be.

"I'm assuming you know my show is not performed by live people then, if you can see them and know what they are?" I just wanted to make sure she understood before continuing.

"Yes, but I don't know how you're doing it or what is happening here." She gestured to Rudy and all around. I'm not sure why I smiled at her confusion. For some reason she looked like a woman who knew everything or coveted truth. My show and my home perplexed her, which for some reason entertained me.

"Off the record?" I doubted she would say anything about my gifts or tell all about my show being performed by ghosts, but I asked anyway.

"Off the record." She nodded, and I knew she would be implicated just as much as I would be if people found out about our powers. The Hero Society had come out to the world without hero identities and mankind was not happy about it. Thankfully, they gave us a second chance and here we were . . . people with gifts could help or not and didn't need to be afraid.

"I control the dead." I don't know what she was thought I would say, but I didn't think my answer was it. Her hand came up to her lips, and she chewed on a fingernail nervously. A bad habit that was cute while taking in my admission.

"What do you mean? You are their puppet master pulling strings?"

"Something like that."

Her finger was out of her mouth and her posture was straight. "No way. You can't just drop that big bomb on me and not go into details."

She was wrong. I didn't have to say anything to a stranger like her. I would eventually, but I was enjoying this moment, and I wanted to make sure I'd get another.

"I can and I am. Tomorrow I have another show, same theater. Come, and then I will talk more. You can take some photos of me all dressed up and run your story on me." I stood and held out my hand for her to take, helping her rise from the stiff couch from the 1920s.

"You're kicking me out and want me to show up tomorrow?" She stood with her backpack in disbelief, her hand not resting in mine, which left a pang of disappointment in my chest. I wanted to touch her, feel warmth from her beating heart keeping her alive.

"Technically you are trespassing. I've been fair. I'd also like to see you again. This is a way to keep the mystery alive." I teased her, hoping she saw it as such instead of me being an asshole. I was known to act like a jerk, but I also didn't have the best people skills.

"Maybe I'll decide you aren't really worth writing a story about, and I suspect you don't have any more to say about the death at your show other than what you reported." She opened the large double doors and gave me one last look that I couldn't tell if she was serious or not. I wished my power had been mind reading instead of controlling ghosts.

"Tomorrow, come to my show." I'd make sure to give her a seat in front where all the magic happened.

She shrugged and tossed her backpack over her shoulder, then began walking down the long driveway to where she parked. I hoped I didn't make a mistake by kicking her out.

Selene Constance wasn't cold, or anything like the women I usually was drawn to, but there was a pull toward her that I didn't understand. I wanted to draw out our time together to figure it out, though.

"Really? She's the first live person we've had in years besides you and you just kick her out so quickly?" Rudy whined from next to me, and I shook my head.

"You'll survive."

"I think I need a hug." Rudy tried to wrap his ghostly arms around me only to have them flow straight through my body. Goosebumps rose against my skin from the chill of the unnatural touching me.

"Let's go rehearse." I turned on my heels, searching for my crew, and a distraction from my drifting thoughts toward Selene.

Chapter Seven
Selene

"I cannot believe you scored us tickets to the show tonight. I mean it was sold out! And I'm pretty sure these are front and center seats!" Emily could barely contain her excitement as we walked together from the parking garage to the theater for Jude's show. How he'd figured out where I lived, I didn't want to know, but this morning there were black roses and a card with two tickets.

I debated whether I should go or not all day, but curiosity eventually won. The journalist in me could not let him and his story go. I had to know the truth and find out every secret he had. I was still working on the Lindsey Walters' case with Echo from the police department and fellow Hero Society members, but there wasn't much to go on right now.

"I have connections." She probably assumed I meant someone through the newspaper, and I wasn't sure I was ready for her screams if she knew they were from Mr. Mallory personally. I still wasn't sure what to make of it all myself.

He was handsome and mysterious, and of course I craved more details on his life and his house. But something felt off, which heightened my interest and made me want to stay away.

"Hopefully everything will be better tonight than what happened at the last show. Have the cops figured out who did it?" Emily was serious now, as we approached the theater with a growing crowd around us.

"Not yet. I'm sure a new clue will surface soon." I tried to be hopeful, but it wasn't looking good. Still, no one was giving up. Lindsey was someone's child, sister, and lover. We couldn't give up on finding the murderer.

We were ushered to our seats, which were in the front of the circular stage. There wasn't anything on the stage, which was confusing since this was like a circus act. Perhaps it added to the mystical part of the show. The lights were off in the middle and every once in a while, I'd see shimmers of blue floating through the darkness. It could be the ghosts or could be light tricks.

"I'm so excited. Work has been so crazy lately, so I needed this night out, and my sister has been driving me nuts."

Emily became the sole guardian of her sister when their parents died. Her sister just started high school and was a pain in the ass. So far, Emily had been doing a good job, essentially as a single parent.

I couldn't imagine what she was going through, but whenever I asked, she said she was fine.

"I'd be happy to watch her some time if you needed it," I offered, not knowing what the hell I would do with a teenager in my small cottage, but I'd give it a shot. Maybe she would just want to watch TV the whole time and order a pizza. I'd be OK with that type of girls' night.

"I appreciate that. It'll be OK. She's just all about boys and being popular and I'm so not that way. We don't exactly see eye to eye." Her green eyes stared at the dark stage, watching the blue light drift higher, then back down again. My friend looked tired and rundown today. Without letting her see, I reached out with my extra gift to make sure death was not surrounding her at all. With her history and mine, we knew the feeling of suicide could sneak up on you even when you weren't in a low.

Nothing. My shoulders relaxed and my whole body settled into the seat. I didn't have a giant crowd of friends, just this pink-haired, green-eyed, petite one beside me and the Hero Society crew when I had time. They were an interesting bunch, and I liked them. They accepted me even with all my flaws.

"Caw!"

The lights over our heads dimmed, and the sound of the godforsaken crow echoed around the room. A spotlight followed it up to a trapeze bar where Jude stood.

"Expect the expected but the closer you look, the more unexpected you see."

I couldn't see Jude's face, just his muscular frame covered in the same black ringleader coat and a top hat. Emily grabbed onto my hand in anticipation, making my shoulder shake slightly from the chuckle escaping my chest. She was such a soft heart. This was not supposed to be frightening, at least I didn't believe so.

"Caw!" The crow came up to its master, then began to dive down toward the stage.

"Prepare for *Mystical*." Jude smirked right before he jumped off the bar, following the bird down to the empty stage. My hand gripped Emily's tighter. There wasn't any landing pad down there. Oh no, he was going to splat on the ground. Gasps and nervous cries echoed around the theater.

"Oh no!" someone screamed, but just as he made it to the floor, he disappeared, like the stage was water and he simply dove into it with his bird. The spotlight stayed on the stage where he'd disappeared for a few seconds while the crowd murmured about what they thought they saw and what they felt happened.

Then the light was gone and we were in darkness. The whole place was silent, as a thrumming from the speakers began, becoming louder and more melodic until suddenly there were shimmering blue people dancing around the stage and one of the trapeze artists from above released his hold and landed perfectly in the middle of the stage with his arm extended and a crow sitting on top.

Jude. What a jerk. Freaking everyone out like that. A talented jerk, but still . . .

I swear he knew what I was thinking because he had a smirk on his face, and he looked more alive than I'd seen him at his house. Our gazes met and I wanted to do something, anything to get back some control of our situation. He didn't win whatever challenge he thought he did by getting me here and freaking me out with his stunts.

So I flipped him the middle finger and he barked out a laugh.

Equipment suddenly appeared. There were people doing tricks and magic all around him. The same small elephant with the young boy played together, tightrope walkers flipped, and jumped on one foot while trapeze artists and aerialists danced in the open air. A tiger jumped through a hoop, and then disappeared only to reappear on top of a box. Now that I was close and paying more attention, I saw that even the few animals on this stage were ghosts except the bird. I didn't know anything other than humans could remain on Earth after death.

The show was spectacular. Jude and his crew put on one hell of a show, and he was right with his opening words to the crowd. Everything they did was expected and looked simple, but the more all of us watched, the more mysterious everything became. I knew the ghosts made a difference.

After ten minutes had passed, the show became a story about a couple in love and the acts of God keeping them apart. I stopped trying to figure out what was happening and just enjoyed it.

Then a blood-curdling scream echoed in the room, and once again, it was not part of the show.

Chapter Eight
Jude

"If you think of anything else you remember about her, please give us a call." The detective who was now assigned to the case of Trixie Long's death gave me a curt nod and walked away.

Another innocent woman was murdered during my show. I knew I was cursed. Fuck, I'd known that since the day I was born, but this was some other curse happening right now.

"She won't talk to me and won't come close. She's very stubborn and isn't ready to let go of the injustice of what happened to her." Selene stepped up beside me where I sat, my head in my hands.

"Maybe I should talk to her." I sighed and stood.

"I don't think that's a good idea. She's mad at you, too. Wrongfully so, but you can't blame her for lashing out right now. If you hadn't had the show, she wouldn't have been here, and why wasn't there more security? Ya know, an angry female rant." Selene was trying to calm me with a bit of humor, but I wasn't in the mood. This night was not supposed to go like this.

The thought made me feel even more pissed at the situation because I should only be thinking about her, and how a poor woman was dead, not that I missed an opportunity to show off to Selene and maybe end with smiles instead of death and blood.

Why the fuck did I want her smiles anyway? I was down to my last month of life. I didn't need her as a distraction.

"I know you're not OK, but you seem extra off. Is something else bothering you?" Her soft fingers touched my arm, and a tingling, shooting sensation spread warmth throughout my skin. I hissed from the shock of pure bliss. I retreated my arm from her touch and looked into her blue eyes.

"You don't know me. You don't know shit about me."

She didn't flinch or arch her delicate eyebrows at me, which only made me feel shittier.

"You're right. I'll be in touch if the paper has anymore need of you." Her expression was completely unreadable. I couldn't tell if she was angry, sad, or cared at all that I was being a dick. I hated this feeling and needed out of here.

I watched Selene walk over to talk with a woman with medium-length black hair and wore a leather jacket. Selene smiled at her, and I felt my chest constrict. Of course, Selene didn't give two shits about me.

"Um, excuse me." A soft female voice spoke from the seats behind me. I turned in the direction with a hardened jaw. But as soon as I saw the shimmering form, I relaxed my face to show empathy.

"You see me, right? Hear me?" The ghost of the murdered woman was there, looking at me like she was unsure I was indeed looking at her or not.

"I do. I'm very sorry about what happened."

"Yeah, yeah. I just knew that I could talk to you for some reason. So here we are, but I think I'm remembering something from before. I'd been asked if I wanted to go backstage and meet you. Of course I said yes, and when I went to grab the pass, I felt a pain in my neck." She reached up to touch her neck where she had felt the pain, but her hand went straight through her shoulder like it was air.

"Do you remember if it was a man or woman who spoke to you?" I wasn't a detective, but I assumed it was the right question to ask. Her ghostly head shook. Damn.

"No, it's very fuzzy." The hand at her neck moved up to her head. She must be feeling phantom pains of a headache. An idea struck me about our problem but I was going to need help.

"Are you . . ." I tried to think of the best way to say what I needed to say without being an asshole.

"Going to move on or stick around for a while?" There really hadn't been another way to say it, so I just blurted it out. Hopefully my words weren't going to send her off into a fit. Her features pinched in and her arms crossed over her shimmering chest.

"I'm not going anywhere, yet. I want justice first. Isn't that a reason you can stay . . . unfinished business or something?"

This woman was stubborn and fiery. Hopefully my idea would work and we'd be closer to catching the killer that has become my new enemy.

"OK. Stay here. Don't wander, and I'll be back tonight to try something that I think could help us both." I looked around to see if people were finished cleaning up and doing their jobs when I saw Selene watching me as I talked with the victim. The burning curiosity inside her blue eyes seduced me. I wanted to feed that monster inside her that yearned for more.

But I'd just been a super ass, and I doubted she would even talk to me now. I deserved her indifference, but this wasn't about me. It's about the killer and bringing peace to the victims and families.

"And I'm gonna bring a friend. The other girl who talks to ghosts." Trixie shrugged.

"As long as she doesn't touch me, I'm good."

That was fair enough, now I just had to convince Selene she could be around me for more than two minutes.

"I'll be back later. I promise." I walked toward a smack in the face waiting to happen.

Chapter Nine
Selene

"I could have picked you up. We were practically driving behind each other." Jude rubbed his hands together, the chill biting into our skin as we walked from the parking lot to the theater doors.

He opened them with a key he magically possessed and held the door open for me to go in front of him. I still hadn't muttered one syllable to the insufferable man, and I was content to keep it up. Whatever mystery I'd been hooked on before with him was gone, ruined by his asshole mouth. Death was something I was around all the time, and it reminded me the future doesn't exist, and we could all die at any moment. I didn't need to give my time and energy to people who didn't deserve it. My time here on Earth was better spent doing things that made me happy, not angry.

"I said I was sorry for the way I acted earlier. I've got stuff happening and these women dying at my show isn't really helping."

I scoffed at his words. Of course these innocent deaths were inconveniencing him.

"Fuck. That came out wrong. Look, I'll explain after we give this a try, OK? Hopefully we can figure out who is killing these women." He spoke with complete sincerity and stepped in front of me. He was sorry. I felt that, and I could see how he could be pissed, then act like a jerk given the circumstances. I'd give him the benefit of the doubt, but that's as far as I would go. Once this whole murder case was solved, I'd leave Jude Mallory to his business and forget all about him.

"OK. Let's do this." I spoke aloud for the first time since seeing him climb out of his black SUV. He closed his eyes in relief before going into the theater seating area.

"I thought you guys weren't going to show. I was coming up with a haunting plan. Talk to you all night while you sleep kind of deal." Trixie sat on the edge of the stage, and I felt a pang of sadness. As much as we needed her to find out what happened in her murder, I know that souls belong onward. Being stuck here when you couldn't feel, touch, or even talk to someone was miserable. Hell, that sort of thing led living people to the doors of death when they were lonely. Ghosts couldn't die again so they just had to learn to deal with it.

"Thank you for sticking around. I really believe this will help." Jude hopped up to sit beside Trixie, and I stood in front of them. He hadn't exactly told me what we were going to try, but he said it was important to the case. He needed my gift to speak to the dead, which he obviously had, too, so I was lost on why I was truly here.

"So what do we do?" Trixie asked, and I looked at Jude expectantly. It was time to reveal this great plan of his.

"I can control the dead. It's my gift. I can make them do as I want, and for a short time I can make them as close to alive as I can. Meaning I can help you get over your dead brain fuzziness and you can tell us what you remember. I need Selene over here to jot everything down and ask the right questions since that is her thing."

Both Trixie and I gaped at the man, who claimed to have vast and extremely powerful gifts over the dead.

"Is that even possible?" I asked. A power like that had to be too much for one person.

"Yeah. My performers are all people who died a century ago. I give them temporary life to do their acts and not be one hundred percent ghost-like. So I know I can help you, but I'm going to apologize now that it is only temporary. I can't bring people back from the dead."

His glanced at me quickly, then back to Trixie. He was lying. Holy hell, he could bring people back from the dead.

"I get it. I'll just be happy to catch this person, then move on. It's no fun staying here alone. I can't even taste a pumpkin spice latte if I wanted to. Now that is hell." Trixie held her hand out toward Jude, and he gave her a sad smile before placing his hand in hers. I knew what to expect, given his words, but seeing his hand clasping onto hers and her ghostly fingers not just sliding through his like she was made of air made me gasp.

"Selene," Jude called out to me, and I nodded. Right. Questions.

"Trixie, is your memory clear?" I whipped out my notebook and pencil, ready to start writing everything down.

"Oh yeah. And I remember the person who asked me if I wanted to go backstage was a female. She had a southern accent, too, like she was from Louisiana or some place like that."

All very good information and was specific enough that it should narrow down suspects.

"Did you notice any of the woman's clothing? Her shoes? Or jewelry?" I looked at Trixie hopeful that she'd seen something noteworthy, but she shook her head.

"She was wearing a cloak. I remember thinking it was all part of the performance. The mystery and all. Her fingernails were painted red. I liked the color." Trixie smiled even though she was remembering her death and the pain. But I bet she was also trying to soak up as many good times in there while she had the chance. Most people after they died didn't get a moment to feel and relive their fondest memories.

"Was there a shimmer to her like the performers on the stage?" Jude looked at me with an arched eyebrow for putting it out there that one of his people could have done it, but I had to think of all options. Now that I knew his power, he could have given all his performers a taste of living again and one of them could have technically done it.

"Let me think. I don't think . . ." She closed her eyes, focusing hard, her eyebrows pinched together from serious effort to remember.

"None of my people would do this," Jude whispered, and I ignored him.

"I think there was a very faint shimmer to her, but it could have been reflecting from the stage. I'm honestly not sure to say a definite yes or no."

"That's OK. You're doing great and you've already given us more than we had before." I tried to make her feel better. I didn't know how long she was going to plan on sticking around, but it wasn't going to be fun being alone thinking that she could have contributed more to this investigation.

"Is there anything else you feel might be important?" We were coming to an end with her memory and Jude stared off into the room like he wasn't even here with us.

"Not right now. I don't remember her, just her voice and the red nail polish. She'd asked if I wanted a pass to go backstage and meet the performers once the show was over. I said yes, and when I reached up to grab the pass, I felt the pain in my neck from the stab." She paused briefly, maybe remembering something else as she recounted the moment of death.

"The knife wasn't silver, though. I would have seen the lights in the show reflecting off of it. Did anyone else say they saw someone talking to me?" She suddenly looked very interested, her eyes wide as they stared at me with hope.

"I'm sorry. No one saw this woman. But that doesn't mean it didn't happen. We are going to figure this out."

"We will bring your killer to justice, Trixie." Jude released his grip on hers and she turned back into a shimmering ghost.

My gaze met Jude's and saw a look in his bright blue eyes of determination. We would figure this out. At least for now Jude and I were on the same team.

Chapter Ten
Selene

Trixie promised to be around in case we needed her for anything but she was also determined to hit the streets, see her family, and try to listen for anymore clues as to who killed her and Lindsey Walters.

Jude was oddly quiet as we walked to our cars.

"Do you know anyone with that description? Accent, female, red nail polish?" I decided to be the one to break the tension that had settled over us. Whether he was a jerk before or not, we needed to work together.

"My performers are from Louisiana, but I do not believe it was one of them. None of them would jeopardize what they have."

He seemed torn, but we couldn't rule them out as a suspect. I needed to talk to Echo, tell her what I learned, and see if she could scent out anything extraordinary in the theater. Maybe Draco would have heard something, too. He knew all the people with gifts in the past, up until fifty years ago when he gave up on his purpose to be the leader of the heroes.

"I think there is more to this story." I meant both with these murders and with him.

"Wanna grab a cup of coffee? I don't feel like going back to the mansion yet." He stopped walking. He looked troubled and tired.

"Tea. I'll join you for tea. I don't drink coffee." There was an open 24/7 breakfast place around the corner and the only place besides a bar open at 11:15 p.m. I wasn't in the mood to deal with lots of people right now.

"OK. Waffle Diner?" He guessed my thoughts and I nodded. Maybe he wasn't in the mood for lots of people either.

"So, you control the dead." I tucked my hands into my sweater pockets. It was getting cooler now that we were in October. Fall was here, and the leaves were beginning to turn to bright oranges, reds, and yellows.

"I do." He shoved his hands in his pockets, too, and we walked toward the diner together.

"Very powerful gift."

"Yeah. Powerful, and comes with a price." He offered the bait, and with the little smirk I saw growing on his lips, he knew he set the perfect trap for me.

"All right, I forgive you for being an ass. Now tell me all about the mysterious Jude Mallory, ringleader of a ghost circus and occupant of a haunted mansion with a giant cemetery in the back." I couldn't help but giggle at the long title I'd just given him, and when he let out a little laugh, I knew the tension he'd brought between us earlier was gone. He was a jerk, but he was hurting and lashed out. Been there, done that, and it was worth giving him a second chance.

"It's a long story."

I think he was giving me an out just in case I really didn't want to hear this long tale of his, but I wasn't budging. I didn't get much sleep these days, anyway. I kept having that feeling like something was gonna happen or like I forgot something I was supposed to do. The nagging sense was hard to push away to rest peacefully.

"Good thing you're getting some coffee and I'm getting some tea."

We made it to the diner and were seated in a booth toward the back. There weren't many people here, yet. But I knew around 2:00 a.m. this place would get busier once the bars closed. We placed our order and waited for our drinks. Once the waitress set them in front of us, I settled into my booth cushion while sipping my tea.

"Storytime," I sang softly, hoping it would ease whatever nervous tension troubled him.

"This isn't going to be published in the paper, right?" His blue eyes narrowed and I shook my head.

"No, this is just between me and you. If it makes you feel any better, I can go into my morbid details, too. Exchange of information." I wasn't ashamed of my past, and what I'd done. I was going insane from not using my powers. I was just grateful to still be here, even on those bad days when I thought I couldn't breathe.

"What's your favorite flower?" he asked randomly.

"Daffodils."

"Interesting choice. I would have taken you for a roses girl." He sipped his coffee, then grimaced. His hand shot out for the packets of sugar and poured them in, along with some creamer. He must like his coffee sweet.

"Daffodils are a symbol of new beginnings, and I am a fan of that." My hands curled around the teacup, warming my skin as I waited for Jude to speak about his life story.

"You know that most superpowers are passed down through family lineage, right?"

"Yes. I know the backstory after the Hero Society spread the knowledge around."

No one in my family had what I had, which wasn't uncommon amongst people with gifts. Sometimes the godly gene traveled through families and sometimes it waited for the right person.

"My particular gifts are strictly passed on from father to son. My family has been in charge of keeping the dead where they belong, in their afterlife. They aren't allowed to speak with mortals or touch them if they stayed instead of passing on. My family keeps that balance. It used to be just a job the family did. When one man died of old age, his son would take his place. But then my great-great-grandfather fucked up." He sipped some more coffee and looked out the window to the dimmed city. He peered past the glass into some painful memory.

"He refused to do his job of protecting mankind. The dead rose from their graves. Ghosts ran amuck, hurting people. The power inside him revolted and cursed my family."

I didn't know how to react. "How do you know you're cursed, and what exactly is the curse?" I wanted to ferret out more answers before calling him crazy and leaving.

"A witch told us. His wife, actually. The power that we have is not a simple power. It's sadly one that comes with a price. We are the protectors who keep you safe from the dead. My great-great-grandfather was killed on Halloween when he turned thirty, torn apart by the souls that had escaped from a dark place. My grandfather was told by his mother that it was our purpose to keep the gates between realms sealed, and his father had paid the price in blood. He brought about the curse on my family. The gene now demands that every man who hosts it, must pay the same price on their thirtieth birthday or the gates will open."

I didn't know what to say. It all sounded nuts, but I did speak with the dead. I knew of the other side and that people couldn't return once they crossed over. Maybe that's because of Jude's family?

Jude. If this was real, then Jude was destined for the same fate as his forefathers.

"Is there a way to break the curse?"

"Yeah. The witch spoke of a way to end the curse."

"And that is?" I swear I was going to have to drag the information out of this man. He was so different than any man I'd met before. He was a walking contradiction. He seemed shy and boyish one minute like he didn't know how to talk to people, then he is this confident Mr. Sexy Pants.

"The gates sealed with thirty years blood paid, a deathly promise be made, until death do you bind shall the curse fade." He recited those words like he'd been saying them over and over since he was born. Maybe he had been.

"That makes no sense."

He sighed and nodded.

"Yeah. No one knew what it meant, and that witch still talks about it like we understand the meaning."

Still talks about it?

"She's alive?"

"She lives in the mansion in her magic room. A ghost, as is everyone else in my family that has passed away. The curse also prevents anyone from moving on until it's broken. So it's kind of high tension at my place around the holidays." He smiled, and I reached out my hand to touch his. To let him know . . . well . . . I didn't know what I wanted him to know. Maybe that I understood . . . sort of.

Instead, I kept my hands to myself and asked a burning question I couldn't stop thinking about.

"So how does the whole circus act fit in?"

Chapter Eleven
Jude

"It's not a circus."

I corrected her, even though my show was mostly a circus. Ruffling her feathers and contradicting her words was becoming something I did often. When she rolled her eyes, I smiled despite the tough topic of my life.

"OK then, ghostly performers that you sort of bring back to life so they can do circus-like acts on a stage. Oh, and with you dressed up in an all-black ringleader suit."

Smart-ass.

"They had been invited to the house to perform for my great-great-grandfather's birthday. When the curse took his life, they got stuck in our family's mess along with everyone else who was there. My family has always let whoever was in the cemetery hang out if they choose to. Some liked the socialization, but now there have been generations of people who can't leave Mallory Mansion."

Her pink lips frowned. She was sad for those who couldn't move on. It was her job to help them move to the other side to peace or silence. The very taste of heaven was in her blood, mingled with a melody of death calling her to those dying or dead.

"I promised them that if they gave me a last year to remember, I would take them with me when I go. We think ghosts and the keeper working together can break the curse. Madam Tully said this year is the year it happens, so it's the only thing we have to go on."

I don't think I'd said my fate out loud to anyone before. It was oddly comforting to know someone else knew the real part of me . . . that I was going to die.

"But what about your family? Don't you have any lovers or children who would want a say in this?" She leaned in closer, her voice more tense than before. I shrugged.

"My family is dead. Each descendent had only one boy and no more. So no cousins that I know of. My mother decided to join my father after he killed himself for the debt to be paid. They raised me as ghost parents but I saw what this curse has done to people. I don't want to put that heavy burden on anyone. No family, no full-time lovers, and definitely no children. When I go, the only thing people will mourn is my show, which is something easy to move on from."

Our waitress came over and refilled my coffee, then asked if we needed anything else. We both shook our heads silently.

"So you only have twenty-eight days to live?" She stared at her tea.

"Yeah. Halloween is my thirtieth birthday." I was thinking about maybe having a party at the mansion, but then decided dying quietly and alone was best. Didn't need anyone else traumatized about finding my body hanging from the tower like I found my father.

"Yep. Trying to go out with a bang of performances." I sipped the newly poured coffee and gagged. This coffee was disgusting. I should have placed my hand over the cup when she came by.

"Here. Try my tea." Selene pushed her cup over toward me, completely trusting.

My fingers brushed hers as I gently pulled the cup over to me and raised it to my lips. It was good, despite not having the same kick that fresh coffee gave me.

"I can see why these murders are upsetting you in more ways than one," she admitted, tucking her hair behind her left ear. She wasn't the type of beautiful woman I'd been with before. She was normal and real, while the others were fake and wanted to be around me because of my notoriety as a magician. They had sculpted bodies from hours at the gym or a surgeon, money-hungry, fame-seekers and cold personalities, like their passionless one-night stands.

"It's not really how I want my show being remembered after I'm gone." I hated to say I, because these women's deaths should be about them, but I couldn't help the way I felt.

"Do you think anyone is purposely doing this to screw up your show? A disgruntled performer or a jealous one because you're getting this life when theirs has ended?"

I wasn't sure.

"Not that I know of. All my performers are happy to hold up their end of the bargain, since I am ending the curse with them, so they can finally leave this place. I don't know why any of them would do anything to anger me."

"OK, what about them having the ability to actually kill someone when you're around? I know souls can't do that normally or at least none that I have come by except . . ." Her face lit up like she'd just figured out something in her head, then her eyes narrowed at me, a conclusion to a mystery I didn't know anything about.

"Someone pushed me down the hill behind your house to the cemetery. I heard laughter and distinctly felt hands push me."

Surrounded by so many ghosts at home drained me after a while, and I never gave them power when I was there. It was against my rules. It created jealousy and rage, and in their excitement someone usually did a lot of damage. I told Selene as much but I wasn't sure if she believed me.

"I know someone pushed me." Her bottom lip was pulled between her teeth as she thought to herself intensely, trying to think of any more clues.

"I believe you. I'm just unsure how that can be true. I am very strict at home. I think that's why my crew like that I am doing this before my end. They get to perform and live again for a few nights. Ralphie gets to feel his elephant's skin and hug him. The trapeze artists feel the energy of the excited crowd."

I hadn't noticed how passionate I was coming off until I noticed Selene intently paying attention to me.

"We'll figure this out. You, me, the Seahill police, and the Hero Society are on it, too."

"I hope so."

A sense of foreboding wiggled its way beneath my skin. Something was different. Not just the feeling in the air as the cold began to settle in

Seahill . . . fall was not the only thing changing the world around us. I looked at Selene and I knew I needed to end whatever was happening before it went any further. The police, the newspaper, and the Hero Society would find the murderer.

"What?" Pink blush coated her cheeks. My mouth opened to speak, to say that I wished her luck on the case and if she needed anything to give me a call, but then she smiled a soft smile like a girl who had a crush.

Fuck, I didn't need this, but I wanted it.

"Nothing. I just think everything is going to be OK."

"It will be," she agreed and took her tea back and lifted it to her perfect light-pink lips.

Chapter Twelve
Selene

Jude and I left the diner late last night, and I still can't believe all the deep information we told each other. Holy hell. His family curse and the fact he has to die to keep the gates sealed, holding back the dead. I even ended up telling him some of my story, about Travis and when I'd gone crazy from not using my powers. He officially knew more about me than anyone, and we'd only known each other for a very short time.

I woke up a little on edge in my head. Maybe it was being around souls so much lately, but the buzz beneath my skin drove me crazy. My thoughts had turned toward the dark, and I couldn't find the will to do anything besides get out of bed for some tea, pee, then get back into bed.

I was grateful I could work from home and did most of the time so I didn't need to fake a smile to anyone today. It wasn't that I had a bad life. Even with my past and my powers, I was still living and doing good. But that's the thing about depression. Somedays it wins, and you need to let it. You need to rest and feel what you're feeling. I'd been to therapy, I'd taken the meds, and what seemed to help me the most was to let it win one day, then push myself back to normal activities the next day. It gave me a deadline for my feelings, and I focused on that instead of feeling like it would never end.

This had worked for me for years to get out of my real lows, but it wasn't for everyone. I wish there was a magic button that cured mental illness, but there wasn't. So today, I read a little from a romance novel I'd been peeking at on my shelf, slept, and watched a show about a witch on TV.

Every once in a while, my thoughts drifted back to Jude. Maybe it was his story that had me falling down the rabbit hole of darkness today, or maybe it was just my time.

I really had enjoyed his show, watching his face light up when he talked about his performance. He told me more about some of his people and their ghost animals that were allowed to move on to where animals go but chose to stay because they loved their caretakers too much. I could see how he appeared to be standoffish in many ways, like he didn't know how to deal with the living. He had been raised by ghosts, his only friends were ghosts, and from what I could tell, the women he had been with for very short moments in his history were nothing more than warm-blooded ghosts.

My parents loved me. They didn't quite know what to do with me when I hit my lows, but they were still there for me. Mom would visit as often as she could when I'd been institutionalized, and Dad would always bring me fresh-cooked dinners when allowed.

Jude didn't have that, which made me want to be closer to him. No one should feel alone, and especially not alone with a fate like his. I still couldn't believe Jude had to die in twenty-seven days! My phone beeped from the other side of my bed, bringing my thoughts back to the present where they belonged.

Echo: We're coming over, and we have junk food.

Today wasn't really the best of days for a get-together, but they were most likely told to come see me by the all-knowing Phillip Griffin.

His sister was a powerful empath and while it was great to be around her, she wandered into my emotions when I was like this. I could see the pain inside her, and I knew if I wanted, she would make me feel happy for a few moments while she was around. But that's not what I needed.

I didn't respond. I didn't feel like peopling earlier than I was supposed to. They'd seen me on my downs, so I didn't have to fake it around anyone of the Hero Society. They just accepted me as I was. I was curious though who was coming over. Echo said "we" so I assumed more than one. There weren't astronomical numbers of members since the Hero Society was still growing and branching out.

The knock on my door came five minutes after the text and I didn't bother putting on a bra before answering the door. My cottage sat on the edge of the city and was small with only two bedrooms. It had a good-sized living room that I filled with a red couch and two black oversized chairs. The kitchen was my dream kitchen with retro-style appliances, and well, the bathrooms were also my favorite. This place was my sanctuary, and I liked to keep it that way. I always felt sad when someone told me their house wasn't their calming, safe space.

"What did you bring?" I asked through the door, peeking through the peephole to see who was on the other side. Apparently, it was just a girls' night.

"The fair is in town so we brought lots of fair food! Caramel apples. Fried Oreos. You must try them," Gwendolyn answered, and I smiled. She was sweet. Hell, they all were.

"All right." I unlocked my door and let the gang of girls into my home.

Rose had a bigger apartment, as did Gwendolyn, for these types of get-togethers but I suspected they were here for me and my mood, to support me and make me feel less alone. I hated to admit it, but the gesture was working already.

Echo was the first in and carried two food boxes in her hand. I always loved the way she carried herself, with confidence and a badass vibe with her medium-length black hair and tanned Native American skin topped off with a signature leather jacket and boots. She had the power to change into any animal she wanted to, and her boyfriend, Asher, was a witch, not from the demigod side of things but wild magic of the Earth. He owned a bar in Seahill with an apartment they shared above.

"I'll grab the plates," she muttered, as she walked in, and got straight to work. Not the best at chitchat, but I had more in common with her than the next woman who danced in. Literally. Lilith was one batshit crazy woman, with long black hair, beautiful brown eyes, and a body any person male or female would crave. She knew it, too. But she was also a retired spy and could take down anyone. She was dangerous but sweet and cared deeply about her friends, me included, thankfully.

Gwendolyn and Rose were the introverts of the group, who I usually hung out with the most. Both didn't handle emotions well, but that didn't stop them from trying to break away from their shy tendencies.

Then there was Esme. She was a nurse who fell in love with the villain who took over the world last year. He loved her, too, and willingly gave up everything to have a chance with her again. If it wasn't for her story, I wouldn't be here now. I had developed a bit of a secret girl crush on her. What she put on the line for love left me in awe every time I thought about it.

"I'm guessing Phillip said you guys needed to stop by?" I closed the door behind them and grinned as I watched them get their sweets and settle in my living room, like they've done many times.

"Nope, we just happened to get lots of food at the fair and think to ourselves, 'Hey, I bet Selene would love some fried Oreos and cotton candy!'" Lilith exclaimed, while Rose became intensely intrigued in her caramel apple instead of looking in my direction. Lilith was not a good liar.

"Right. So I'm sure one of you has an agenda for tonight. What are the plans?" The girls had girls' night frequently as a way to destress from the whole "saving the world gig" and getting away from their intense men. However, they did love their men with every fiber of their being. Separation was good for them from time to time, which was fine with me. It was sometimes hard being in a room with six perfectly matched soul mates. The sexual tension and love vibes were crushing.

"We were thinking maybe we'd just hang, chat for a bit, then watch a movie. Eat all the goodies. The men said they can handle the city tonight," Echo answered and a few of the girls snickered at the thought of the boys handling the city without them. We all knew they were perfectly capable of it. I mean you had Draco, who used to be a general in an ancient Greek army turned immortal with another man who had super speed and strength. Add a witch, and a man who could manipulate water, then finally a villain turned to the good side, who happened to be the only demigod left in existence. I think they were good, but the gals still gave them shit.

As I sat down, I thought about what it would be like to have someone to smile with, laugh with, and also be serious and intense. Someone to have hot sex with . . . something that had been lacking for a while.

Jude flashed into my head when I thought about sex, but then I pushed the thought away. He only had a month to live, and as fun as I knew it would be, I wasn't sure I wanted to hurt my heart.

Jude

"So how's it going with Miss Reaper?" Rudy plopped his ghostly ass onto the couch beside me as I fiddled with a deck of cards in my hands.

"Fine. Hopefully we can help in some way to solve the murders at my show. You haven't heard any of the others talk about killing anyone or being pissed at me for something, have you?" I still didn't think it was my crew, but there wasn't any harm in asking the biggest gossiper of the group. If anyone was contemplating murder, Rudy would know about it.

"Nope. None of us are wanting to fuck up our only chance of moving on."

Frustrated, I knew he was right.

"Have you guys been feeling different at all? Selene said she felt someone push her into the cemetery. It wasn't me, but it shouldn't have been any of you, either."

Rudy shook his head so quickly, it turned around like an owl's would. Sadly, I wasn't even fazed by the movement, having been so used to antics like that since I was a kid.

"I think you would know very quickly if we were able to actually touch things and move them. You probably would wake up with Lucy's mouth on your cock if that were true."

I groaned, as the she-devil walked in, as if she waited until someone said her name.

This was not a conversation I wanted to have. I just needed some alone time to think, which was not a common occurrence in a house where doors did not keep people from coming into your room to interrupt the peace.

"I'm going for a walk," I announced to the room, and the two beings occupying it wisely didn't question my sudden change.

As I walked through the halls of the mansion aimlessly, I tried to empty my mind and be like the ghosts around me, drifting through the world. I didn't know what to do about the murders right now, and I wanted to see Selene again but didn't know what to do about that, either. Neither of us needed this flimsy friendship to turn into anything more than what it was, and the more time I spent with her, the higher percentage of that happening would occur. She was smart and a smart-ass. She was fun to be around, talk to, and yeah she wasn't my typical type of woman, but she was stunning.

Despite wanting to be alone, I shuffled my deck of cards all the way to Madam Tully's room in the basement. A candelabra waited on a shelf at the bottom of the stairs with a light for me. There wasn't any electricity down here.

Like the rest of the house, the basement was not normal. It was just as artfully decorated with no amount of cash spared. Artwork and curtains hung from the ceiling to the floor with lush carpets that could use a good vacuum. The whole place was stuck in the early 1800s, including some of its inhabitants. Although, most ghosts didn't wander down here, since the lack of light reminded them of being underground in a grave or in a coffin. I also heard from Rudy that Madam Tully made them uncomfortable. She was a witch who married into the family and had originally warned her husband about the repercussions of not doing as he was born to do. Some of the ghosts believed she could have done more to stop the curse, but I didn't. We only had control of ourselves in this life. What other people did was not our fault.

"Prince of Souls, why so sad and full of woe?"

I rolled my eyes as I pushed the intricately carved wooden door to see the witch's ghostly head inside a crystal ball.

"I hate it when you try to rhyme. It makes you sound crazy."

The ancient souls say the mansion was built on sacred ground and was a hub of wild magic fought over for many years. Many deaths occurred. Madam Tully's room was a place of worship to that wild magic. She had an altar and plants that were still alive despite never seeing sunlight and I doubted she had watered them in over a century. Two elegant high back seats sat by a table in the front with a deck of tarot cards and a crystal ball more for show than functional, and the walls were lined with various symbols, statues, and crystals of every color imaginable.

"Crazy I may be, but there is more than what you see."

I sat down in the only chair that wasn't dusty, since my ass was in it more frequently than not.

"I've got a lot going on in my head," I admitted, relaxing for a little bit. I couldn't talk to anyone else, even my ghostly family. Mom and Dad were still all about each other and liked to take vacations around the cemetery to get out of the house. Everyone else did whatever they wanted, not caring about the living except for my performers. Even with them, I felt they humored me because I said I would take them into the afterlife once the curse was broken.

Madam Tully liked my company and was always there if I needed to vent or get advice. She knew about the future but would never tell specifics.

"What's going on?" She gave up the theatrics and pulled herself out of the crystal ball to sit in the chair opposite of me.

"I'm cursed, and people are dying at my show." I didn't mention Selene because I didn't think there was anything to tell.

Madam Tully arched her eyebrow and pursed her lips. Her hair was straight, and she was a healthy woman when alive, with womanly curves and proud of it. When she first married, she had been about Selene's size but she was unhappy, later in their marriage she embraced who she truly was and let her inner goddess come out. I envied her acceptance of herself most days. She kept it real while everyone else played it safe.

"You sure the curse will end with me?" Even if my deal with my performers turned out to be nothing, I had no heir to continue the line of gatekeepers.

"It will, that much is clear, but there is still so much that needs to be done. Something has changed in the Earth. Souls are slipping out of places they should not be, gaining abilities they are not allowed to have."

"What do you mean?"

One side of her lips tilted upward as she raised her hand toward a glass coated in dust and webs.

I didn't understand what she was trying to demonstrate until her fingers connected with the glass, and it tumbled toward the ground, shattering into little crystal pieces all over the floor.

"Impossible." I couldn't take my eyes away from the broken glass shimmering in the candlelight. I hadn't given her the ability to touch the glass, to move it. I'd always been very careful in the house to keep my powers contained to me. If she was able to do that, then . . .

"My dear Jude, impossible has now entered the realm of possible."

Chapter Thirteen
Selene

Despite two people being killed at Jude's last two shows, the tickets were sold out for tonight's performance. Due to the added hype, people wanted to be there. Conspiracy theories circulated about the murders being part of the show. Either the murders weren't real or he helped the girls escape horrible lives by faking their deaths with his magic. Everyone wanted to see what was going to happen next.

This time I was not here for fun or to watch Jude on the stage. Undercover police agents were scattered in the crowd as well as unmasked Hero Society members. All of us were here to hopefully catch the killer.

I hadn't heard from Jude besides shooting him an email that I would be there shortly. He already knew about the undercover cops. Soon after, ten tickets popped into my inbox from him, along with his number that I put into my phone immediately. Now all we could do was wait and keep our eyes open. The show was going to start in about eighteen minutes, and I prayed no one got hurt tonight.

"Excuse me, Ms. Constance. Mr. Mallory wants to see you backstage." A stagehand with a headset over his blond hair looked at me with an impatient brown-eyed stare.

I nodded and stood. This person didn't look like the description of the killer Trixie had given, and her ghost glared to determine if he was the one. She gave me a shake of the head before drifting off to maybe catch a glimpse of the person somewhere else in the crowd.

There was chaos backstage with the ghost performers getting ready. They looked more real close up, and I was tempted to reach out and touch them. They still had that shimmering blue glow to them, but they looked more solid, like my hand wouldn't go through them.

"Mr. Mallory." The stagehand alerted our presence, then went off in the direction of the trapeze artists. A few eyes watched me as I stood before their leader. I noticed one of the trapeze ladies giving me the stink eye and the male an appreciated glance.

My head turned toward Jude, dressing in his ringleader suit with a big top hat on his dark hair. He looked jazzed, like he was ready to run around the room, like a commander ready to go off to battle. My tummy fluttered in response. There was dark liner under his eyes, making the blue in them pop. His jaw was sharp.

"Oh good, you're here."

He stopped pacing and walked up to me, hands cupping my jaw, and suddenly his lips clashed against mine.

I was stuck, frozen against his hard body. My eyes widened in shock. I didn't know if I should push him away, but the more his unyielding mouth caressed mine, his tongue asking permission against the seam of my lips, the more I kissed him back. His touch lit my senses ablaze. Death kissed me and I never felt more alive. My eyes closed, and my hands went to the black lapels of his coat, pulling him closer. The need to feel more and take more consumed me. Strong hands moved down my neck, over my ribs, then gripped behind my thighs, lifting me up against him to wrap my legs around his body.

I didn't know what the fuck was happening, but I couldn't stop. His kiss was like a drug, and I couldn't pull away from the sweet bliss running through my veins. He walked us somewhere, then closed a door behind him. I didn't want to drag my lips away from his to look. Whatever he wanted from me, I was very willing right now. My mind felt numb, like he gave me a shot of Novacaine to my thoughts with every nip at my bottom lip.

"I think we're good," he whispered against my mouth and I nodded. I was good, absolutely good.

His hands eased from my body, and his kiss pulled away from me.

"I needed to talk to you without anyone knowing. I'm using my powers to keep them away from this room."

Jude said what? My eyes flew open and burning hot fire coated my insides. He kissed me because he needed to talk to me privately?

"I'm sorry I kissed you to get us in here, but I don't trust anyone right now. Some, if not all the ghosts in this realm, have abilities I didn't give them. They can touch things, move them, even kill."

Oh, I was livid as fuck right now. I felt used, and hurt. I enjoyed kissing him. I wanted more of what he had to give, and it was only an excuse to talk to me. The numbness, the sweet bliss inside my soul became cold and painful.

"How do you know this?" I managed not to have a bite to my voice, but Jude still grimaced. I'm sure despite trying not to appear affected by what just happened, my face didn't listen.

"Madam Tully, the witch ghost in my basement, showed me, then warned me she wasn't the only one who could do these things. Plus you said someone pushed you into the graveyard. It wasn't me so it was someone else. And none of the ghosts at my home has said anything. The killer could be anyone . . . my crew or some other ghost with a vendetta."

"How?" Too many emotions rolled through my head, and I was having trouble latching onto a single thought. This was all so confusing. I'd never met a soul who could make physical contact with me, until I met Jude and he revealed his power. I could always touch them, but now he was telling me they could touch me without his gift of helping them do so.

"I don't know, but if a soul can touch you and disappear as they normally do, then we are screwed." His tan fingers ran down his face in frustration. He was right, and I was afraid. A ghost with the ability to touch and then vanish made the perfect assassin. Music vibrated through the walls, and I looked at Jude cautiously.

"I have to go, but be careful." His gaze dropped to my lips. I felt the hunger in that look that he wanted to kiss me again, but instead he turned to open the door and left for the stage.

Chapter Fourteen
Selene

I avoided the stares from the ghostly crew when I exited the room. Their side glares made me feel cheap, like they all thought I let him have his way with me in there, which only made the heat in my cheeks burn hotter. I would have let him take me in that room. I felt like an idiot falling for his stupid kiss the way I did. He was just so intense, and the sensations he stirred in me were something I'd never felt before.

"Don't get attached." One of Jude's female performers blatantly glared at me while drawing a heart on her cleavage above her corset. She was gorgeous, and in her living days, would have been a heartbreaker for sure. Now she was only a shimmering ghost of her former self.

I didn't need to say anything to her or any of the other performers. As I walked away, I thought about her voice, and Trixie's killer. My gaze drifted back toward her hands looking for red nail polish but I only saw the shimmering blue coating of her whole body.

"He's mine," she mouthed and my instincts screamed danger. I'd be keeping an eye on that performer the whole time, just in case the red flags going off in my head were accurate. Jealousy could definitely be a motive, especially when the victims wanted to be near Jude.

I passed Draco as I went back to the seat before the stage.

"Jude says some of the dead can act without his powers now," I warned him and he only nodded his head. Draco was big and strong. His long brown hair and beard gave him a casual appearance but he was a leader. Born thousands of years ago, he has lived through everything. The air around him vibrated with a confidence only an ex-immortal could have.

"Be careful." His gruff voice reached me as I walked by to the only open seat in the place.

The lights dimmed as soon as I reached my seat, and I looked for Trixie. It had to be hard for her, seeing this whole production with performing ghosts able to touch and be almost alive for a night when she couldn't.

At the first caw of the crow, my gaze darted back to the stage.

"What is life beyond death, if not the greatest adventure into *Mystical*."

Lights lit up the stage as a woman is cut by a guillotine. Her body rose and her head looked around the room with a smile on her face. It was eerie, and many in the crowd gasped, some even screamed from terror. But everyone sat in their seats, waiting and uncompromisingly watching for what would happen next.

Jude appeared under a spotlight, just in front of the woman's decapitated head, and lifted it gently to her. The crowd's energy was electric, yet there was no sound beyond the footsteps of the ringleader. A tiger growled and prowled toward the woman and Jude as she placed her head back on her neck.

"Is this life or death, you may ask, but the truth is. . ." Jude turned his body, directly facing the audience with his eyes on me.

"You're already in the mystical adventure of death." He smirked as the tiger leaped, his bared teeth aiming for Jude's exposed back. My fingers went up to my mouth to stifle the scream just as the tiger collided with his body and they both turned into butterflies.

I was going to need his secrets on how he did all his tricks. It was such a mystery. Trapeze artists flew and flipped together in the air. The woman who hissed that Jude was hers walked one foot at a time on a tightrope, then flipped onto a horse that appeared out of nowhere with Jude on its back. Her hand wrapped around him possessively and my gaze narrowed at the gesture.

"It wasn't a real kiss," I whispered to myself, trying to focus on the show for anything stranger than ghosts performing. With great effort I tore my gaze away from Jude and looked around the crowd for the killer. Trixie was doing the same. Out the corner of my sight, I noticed someone walking toward me, covered in a hood.

Draco moved from his spot against the wall and began walking toward me, with his focus on the hooded person. Trixie disappeared from her perching spot, then appeared next to Draco. Both of them didn't want to spook the killer.

"You're wanted backstage." A feminine voice spoke to me, and a pale hand with red polish lifted beneath the large sleeve of the hooded cape for me to take it. I tried to see who was beneath the hood, but only saw a bluish shimmer, giving them away as a soul and nothing else.

"I don't think so," I whispered, as a woman behind me told the stranger to move out of her way.

"If he falls for you, then you're gonna die. Remember that, Reaper. I won't be the only one out for your head." The voice morphed into a gurgling noise, and Trixie appeared before the figure and lifted the hood.

Nothing. The hood dropped to the ground as if there had been nothing beneath it but air.

"Hey, sit down! We can't see!" someone behind me hollered, and I realized I'd risen to my feet. I was too hyped to stay there and finish watching the show. I knew the hooded ghost had been the killer. I felt its dark aura, the aura of someone who had taken a life. That kind of stain on a soul doesn't go away, it rots, and creates a fate of misery. Even before the woman had become a ghost, she'd hurt someone.

"Let's go," I told Trixie and Draco. We needed to get out of view and keep an eye out for the killer in case she wanted another victim since she didn't get the chance to kill me. We made it to the side of the building where Phillip stood, watching. He was tall, handsome, but unlike Draco, he had blond hair and looked more boyish. He was dangerous in his own way, though. He knew all the possible future outcomes, and when you know the future, you can bet on whichever one played to your advantage. He'd done it once before . . . bet the lives of everyone, even his sister if Rose's retellings of the big battle were true. He would do whatever had to be done for what he deemed as the best future.

"The killer is a ghost, but I didn't see a face. Just the same pale hand and red polish Trixie saw." I was frustrated. Every one of them was transfixed on the performance onstage. Jude was getting the performance he wanted without murder occurring, but I couldn't get the sinking feeling in my stomach to disappear despite the deep breaths I started to take. I hadn't felt fear with the killer near. After having spent time with Jude backstage, I figured I'd be a target like the other women. However, that feeling in my tummy only seemed to harden and churn when I repeated the woman's words over and over in my head. *If he falls for you, then you're gonna die. Remember that, Reaper.*

I didn't think I'd have to worry about Jude falling for me. He was against love and relationships, since he was destined to die in twenty-seven days. She'd also mentioned the title of Reaper, so she knew who and what I was, and there wasn't any fear in her tone. There were only one set of ghosts that knew I couldn't take them onward.

My nervous gaze lifted to where Jude danced across the stage, pulling magic out of his hat surrounded by ghosts who could kill a live person, including him.

Chapter Fifteen
Jude

The performance proceeded perfectly, and nobody died. I was riding the high of a successful show that I told my ghosts to go back to the mansion and enjoy the wine in the cellar. I'd let them feast and feel for the night. All of them disappeared, and I felt their presence in the mansion even from the stage. The mansion and I were connected. The gate to the afterlife was bound to me by blood and birthright. I thought about joining them. Instead I walked toward the crowd that waited by the stage with Trixie.

"This night's show was perfect!" I announced as I neared Selene and her friends, although my steps slowed the closer I got. They weren't excited or joyous as they looked at each other nervously.

"What happened?" I took a step next to Selene and while it was a small movement, she leaned away from me. I'd thought after the hell of a kiss we shared earlier that she'd want to be near me like I felt toward her. I'd wanted to talk to her and to tell her about what I'd learned. Instead, as soon as I saw her, I couldn't think about anything else beyond tasting her lips. It was stupid to want her, knowing I would die in a few weeks. Maybe she didn't enjoy our kiss, despite how passionately she kissed me back. If it wasn't for the show and the pressing matter of the barrier to the otherworld deteriorating, I would have stayed in that room with her, exploring her lips and the whimpering sounds she made when I nibbled against her skin.

"The killer showed up and wanted Selene." Trixie broke the silence with a shrug. I glanced over her face, then her body, looking for signs of an injury. She wasn't dead, so I called that a win, but everyone's faces looked pinched.

"I'm Phillip. This is Draco, our leader of sorts, and this is Echo. She works for the Seahill PD and for us."

A tall blond man stepped forward and pointed to the two others with him. A muscular man with brown hair and a beard reeked of an ancient soul. He had seen many deaths in his lifetime. Echo I'd seen before, her black medium-length hair and scowl hadn't changed since our first meeting at the first murder during my show.

"Nice to meet you all. Now bring me up to speed, please." My mind hadn't moved passed the killer wanting Selene. Right now all I cared about was that someone tried to hurt Selene.

"The hooded figure came and said I was wanted backstage. She had the same red polish and pale skin like Trixie said but I noticed the blue shimmer underneath the hood. I couldn't see any other type of facial features. It was like she wore a mask or something." Selene talked while avoiding my probing stare. I wanted her to look at me, to see me, to confirm that the kiss we shared wasn't all an act.

"Anything else?"

"She did say something else before Trixie tried to rip off her hood." Again, Selene wouldn't look at me and the others watched us. An uneasy vibe settled over the group.

"Yeah. She said . . ." Selene struggled to get the words out. She was afraid to say them, which intrigued me.

"Oh, for fuck's sake. She said, 'If he falls for you, then you're gonna die. Remember that, Reaper. I won't be the only one out for your head.'" Echo exhaled impatiently.

"But we don't need to worry about that, so good news, I'll survive." Selene tried to wave off the warning, however all her jittery announcement did was make the group feel awkward. She and I needed to hash some things out but first we needed to talk business with the Hero Society.

"Do you have any ideas on who the killer is?" I kept my professional mask of ringleader as I looked at the superhero clan.

"Unless there is a very convincing cross-dresser underneath that hood, I think it's safe to say the killer is a woman. A ghost woman. She has been picking people that have caught your attention or are interesting in seeing you, such as Trixie here. A fan. Motive seems to be jealousy, but that can't be confirmed. We're going to need to keep digging and possibly interview your crew. Selene said that might be possible, since she can talk to them."

Echo divulged the bullet points on the case of the killer, and I tried to think of someone in my group of ghosts that would do something like this. Lucy, instantly popped into my head, but then I pushed the thought away. She wanted to sleep with me, but she wasn't in love with me. She just missed the comfort of a warm body and the emotional connection between two people. Hopefully she would sleep with another ghost tonight and fill her sensation quota.

"Anything I can do to help. I'll make them talk if I have to." Since I was destined to die, I might as well do something other than wallow about my shitty fate and isolation.

"I think it's an excellent idea! Selene, talk it over with Jude and let us know when and where. Echo and Rose will assist you in the interviews." Phillip grinned and clapped his hands together excitedly. Then his hands grasped around his friends' arms and pulled them away slowly.

Strange exit, but maybe that was normal and I just didn't know. Dealing with the dead was easier than the living for me. A sigh from beside me brought my attention back to Selene. She avoided eye contact with me.

"What's wrong? I mean facing death can make people upset but you're with death all the time." My hand started to lift toward her chin, but then I chickened out and dropped it. The women I'd been with before were cold and their emotions were buried far beneath the surface. Selene wore hers on the outside. I saw and felt her confusion like it was my own.

"I'm trying to sort my head out, that's all," she answered and I looked up to Trixie for any clues as to what Selene's troubles were but she shrugged and disappeared.

"Talk to me, Selene." The need to touch her defeated my uncertainty of our feelings, whatever the hell they were called. My fingers caressed her cheek and her hand jerked up to smack my touch away from her soft skin.

"I'm hurt, OK? Not that I almost died, but you kissed me so you could talk to me. You couldn't have just grabbed my hand and pulled me into the room? You had to kiss me with your stupid death-weaved lips."

I know I apologized for kissing her to get her away from the crowd, but she didn't honestly believe that was the reason I kissed her, right? I couldn't think of anything else at the time more than I needed her lips.

"You really don't believe that I only kissed you to get you in that room, do you?" I dared her wrath as I reached out again. This time my fingers went beneath her chin to lift her gaze to mine.

"That's what you said, so what else should I have believed?" Her voice rose and the pain she'd felt from our interaction came to the surface. However, she didn't move her face from my touch or my stare.

"I'm sorry for that. I've lived with the dead for so long that I've forgotten how to act amongst the living." It was a sad excuse but it was the only one I had at the moment.

"When I saw you, all my focus leveled on your lips. It's stupid to want to touch you, and I acted purely on instinct. I enjoyed the kiss, enjoyed feeling you beneath my fingers, against my tongue. I know it's stupid to act upon those things considering I only have a few weeks to live and the murders occurring, but I want to do it again."

Her lips parted and my body pulled into the gravity of her touch. Something lay there, hidden beneath the surface of this thing between us. Something I'd never felt before but couldn't stop as we drew closer and closer, even if I burned in the end.

Chapter Sixteen
Selene

So many emotions and words came to my mind, but none found their way past my lips. Should I believe him? The way his lips parted and eyes peered at me with longing pointed toward the truth in his admission. But what about everything else?

"I'm not asking you to marry me, Selene, I'm asking you to let me kiss you. But if you don't wanna get involved, then I understand." His hand dropped from my chin, and the cold feeling from his stepping away brought a shiver to my skin. I wanted to kiss him, but my head wasn't clear.

"What about the killer's threat?" I pulled my bottom lip between my teeth and watched his expression change from the indifferent mask he'd put on for defense to a smirk.

"I haven't fallen in love with anyone yet. I doubt it'll happen in the next twenty-seven days. No offense."

It may sound harsh coming from him, but my shoulders sagged from the relief of his words. I didn't have time for something serious, and while I knew I deserved love, I didn't feel like I was ready for it. My hands shook as they lifted up to his chiseled jaw.

"Whenever I'm around death, I get this sort of tingle beneath my skin. The closer I get, the more euphoric the sensations become. Kissing you was like tasting the warm lips of death." I figured his truthful words needed an admission of my own, something I'd never told anyone about being drawn to the bliss of death in a sensual way.

"Makes sense. I am the master of the dead."

His head tilted as he pressed a gentle kiss to my hand, sending a shiver from my fingers to my toes.

"There is something else there, though, isn't there?" There was a nagging sensation, like fingers caressing a closed door, trying to be welcomed in.

"I don't care right now." His hand held my face still as he bent to kiss me. This wasn't like the surprising kiss we'd had before. There wasn't any clashing of teeth and tongues the moment our lips met. His touch seared my senses and burned its way into my soul, branding the imprint of his kiss on my heart. It was a slow, patient kiss, like we didn't have only twenty-seven days to explore this thing between us but like we had thousands of years. His breath blended with mine with every intake, invading my lungs and my body as if he could ingrain himself in my very blood.

Death kissed like he'd waited all of eternity for this moment, and he would take his time enjoying every sensation. My knees weakened, and my hand had moved to the back of his neck, keeping his head rooted in place, his lips pressed against mine. Every breath felt heavy, as my nerves lit up with every sensation of his warm body touching the front of mine.

"Your kiss is heaven." His growl reverberated down my throat and shook my heart.

"Peace." I breathed against his lips, feeling the type of peace I'd only felt on the edges of the glowing afterlife. "Peace. You taste like internal peace." I pressed his lips once more to mine, then parted our connection. His forehead rested against mine as we calmed our erratic beating hearts and basked in the tranquility of the moment.

"Do you wanna come back with me to the mansion for a tour? We can talk to some of the ghosts as we pass by." His body straightened as his fingers caressed my cheek, then my wet lips, feeling the evidence of what we had shared.

I smirked. "This isn't you trying to get me to come home with you so I'd bone you, right?"

"A gentleman would never do such a thing," he scoffed playfully, which made a tiny giggle burst from me. I doubted Jude Mallory was a gentleman. Instead, he looked devilishly mysterious, a trait I hadn't experienced before in the opposite sex but now found attractive. Now that I'd cooled down from the anger I had before, a carefree sensation and eagerness to live in the moment took over me. I wouldn't sleep with Jude tonight, but I wouldn't mind spending more time with him.

"We'll see about that." I nodded toward the door and Jude's face lit up with his smile. The expression made his very handsome face of a man appear boyish. I liked that look on him. Everything he'd told me about his life told me it hadn't been easy. Parents' suicide, then raising him as ghosts, plus knowing he has to die in a few weeks, probably by his own hands. Heavy, heavy burdens rested on his shoulders and I doubted he had many opportunities to shake them off.

"Do you want to ride together or drive there yourself?" he asked, as we started walking toward the exit. The cleaning crew were getting started on their jobs so I'm glad we were leaving.

"I rode with Phillip, who left me . . ." I stopped the rest of the words from coming out of my mouth when a thought clicked in my head. Without warning, my shoulders trembled and a bark of laughter came barreling past my lips. Jude stopped to stare at me with wide eyes, having no clue what brought on my sudden fit of amusement.

"That sneaky son of a bitch. He asked me to ride with him on purpose." I had thought it was weird that Phillip invited me to ride with him, though I didn't think much of it. He was friendly and passing by my little cottage, so why not? Of course, he only did it because he knew this thing between Jude and I would happen and that I'd be invited to go back to Jude's mansion with him. He left abruptly, and I had been so caught up in my emotions, I totally forgot that he'd been my ride until now.

"I'm kinda lost here." Jude smiled, then a small chuckle bubbled up from his chest when I had a laugh attack in front of him.

"Oh, you must not know. Phillip, the blond guy you met? He sees all the possible futures and likes to help things happen the way he thinks would lead to the optimum future for all. He invited me to ride with him to the show because he knew this would happen and I'd have no ride if he left. Apparently, I'm supposed to go with you."

It sounded wild and almost like I needed a tin foil hat to say it aloud, but I knew how Phillip worked. I'd chatted with the guy, heard the stories from the ladies of the Hero Society. He told his sister to take a walk in the woods when a storm blew in and she had to hide in a stranger's chicken coop. Of course, the chicken coop turned out to belong to Draco.

"I'm liking the man more and more." Jude winked and grasped onto my hand, leading me toward the doors to where his vehicle waited to take us to his haunted mansion.

Chapter Seventeen
Jude

Selene sat comfortably in my sports car as I drove us farther and farther away from the skyscrapers and city lights. We didn't really speak as time passed by. She watched the buildings turn to trees like the sight was the only thing that mattered in the world to her.

It was nice to be around a woman who didn't balk at the idea of being so far from the metropolitan area. Not that I'd brought any women to my home because having a ghost do weird shit while you tried to fuck would kill the mood. But whenever I'd mention to them that I didn't have a flat in one of the tall towers, and I had my mansion in the woods, a sneer would appear on their naturally sour expression.

The longer we rode, the more I thought about how fucking depressing my life had been, and because I knew I would die, I forgot to truly live. By the time we drew near the entrance to my driveaway, my mood had darkened.

"Who are they?" Selene pointed toward four shimmering figures standing outside the gates to my home.

"Idiots." I rolled my eyes at the four ghosts dressed in Victorian-era clothes with suitcases packed and their thumbs sticking up to hitch a ride. They knew that they couldn't leave the property. They had already walked as far as the curse would let them go. Even my crew had to come back after I was done with them, like they were all tied by a cord to the house. They could try to escape but would eventually be yanked back to their personal purgatory.

"Are they hitchhiking?" They moved out of the way as I turned into the road and pressed the button for the gates to open for us.

"Yes, we're heading to New Mexico!" Roger, one of the ghosts, popped into my car. His grotesque corpse-like face made Selene let out a surprised scream.

"Never gonna happen, buddy," I told him as we drove to the side of the property where I'd had a carport built to keep the sun off my car.

"How do you do, my lady?" Roger's ghostly hand appeared out of thin air and tipped the frayed hat that sat on his head.

"Nice to meet you?" She chewed on her bottom lip nervously, and I felt my cock stir from the sight of her flesh between her pearly teeth.

"Oh, it's nice to meet you. Won't you take us when you leave? We won't bother you or ask to go to the bathroom. Really we are the perfect traveling companions." Theodore, another of the ghosts, appeared in my car as I put it in park.

"You know you gentlemen can't leave, so get out of my car. You're making it smell like desperate ghost in here."

"You were such a nice boy as a kid. Age has not been kind to you." Theodore stuck out his tongue like a child, then he and his friend disappeared. I could have made them leave, but as a rule I tried not to control the dead too much. My work with the performers was enough to let my power out. If I didn't release some of that energy, I'd go crazy, and I didn't have room for that on my agenda before my upcoming death.

"This is going to be interesting, isn't it?" Selene asked as a smile grew on her face, and I nodded. I hadn't brought anyone here before, so I'm sure she would get loads of attention and curious stares.

"It's not gonna bother you, is it?" A gnawing worry grew in my thoughts that this experience would be too much for her. She said she reacted differently around death, and this house held a lot of death. The house was too big and decorated to show how rich my ancestors had been. It wasn't a home filled with family portraits or knickknacks. It had bustles of poets and stoic-faced paintings of rich people of the past. Purples, greens, and golds weaved into every room to show a high-class status for the people who would dine and party every night.

I hadn't realized I'd gotten stuck in my thoughts until a warm hand caressed my trimmed beard. Selene looked at me with understanding. Her blue eyes were a trap for my soul, a place I could lose myself in. I'd known it since the first time I saw her in that crowd. Death permeated from the slain girl, and Selene stood there like a light in the dark, without fear and judgment. A simple understanding that no one could feel but us. Two souls ruled by death.

"It'll be fine. I don't scare easily." Her fingers ran up my jawline, then caressed my cheekbone and settled against my lips. A consuming desire to kiss the fuck out of her came over me.

"If you don't wish to be ravaged in this car, then we need to get out," I said, unable to voice my words calmly. Something about her made me feel possessive and selfish. I wanted to feel her lips on mine again, her creamy skin beneath my fingers, and her moans against my mouth as I slid between her legs slow and hard.

Her lips parted and my fingers gripped the material of my black pants to keep from wrapping around her neck and pulling her mouth to mine.

"Not a lot of room in here. I think we better get out." She leaned in as she spoke, her sweet breath grazing my lips. Suddenly she climbed out of the car without a glance back at my restrained posture. *What the hell was wrong with me?* Two kisses from Selene and I suddenly transformed into a caveman who wanted nothing but to carry her to my cave and fuck.

Twenty-nine years. I'd gone twenty- nine years without behaving like this, and instead of spending the rest of my short life enjoying the fame and performances, my thoughts were consumed by Selene.

She began walking up the steps when I'd exited the car and caught up to her. Since people never came here, I rarely locked the door, so I let us in without the jingling of keys to let the ghosts know someone was coming in.

Performers were cheering and enjoying their night of fun and feeling. Lucy made out with both of the trapeze performers in the foyer. Selene's eyebrow raised and I sent a little zap of power to the threesome to take it somewhere more private. Lucy pulled back and licked her lips at me, the invitation to join obvious in her stare, but then her sultry eyes saw Selene and narrowed. She sneered at the sight of the two of us, grabbed onto the two lovers, then disappeared together. I saw the hurt and jealousy. I knew she wanted me in her bed, but I'd assumed she just wanted to feel a warm body, but her clenched jaw and angry stare indicated she wanted more from me. They weren't things I could give her, which made her situation more depressing.

Selene broke the awkward tension. "After I left the room with you earlier, she told me not to get attached to you, and that you were hers."

"I don't think she's capable of killing someone." Lucy could be a pain in the ass and spoiled, but the energy around her wasn't vicious. Mischievous maybe, but I'd never picked up on anything dangerous.

"She has motive that's for sure. She's in love with you." Selene shrugged, then walked farther into the house, observing the expensive furnishings, and celebrating ghosts floating around.

"She's been with every single one of the men in my family while they were alive since she died, even my dad. I didn't want to follow that particular family tradition." I had a desire to touch Selene's hand, to hold it gently in mine. The ghosts in the house continued to talk and interact, but they would occasionally look toward our approaching forms. Without thinking more about it, I clasped her hand in mine, staking claim that she was mine and protected in this place. My trust within my home had diminished once Madam Tully showed me that the ghosts around me had powers but hadn't said anything. One could easily have slit my throat while I slept and the uneasy feeling in my head acknowledged that if the curse didn't exist, a ghost would have tried it by now.

"You said you like to read, right?" I needed to get back to the moment of me and Selene.

"Yeah, I do." She glanced down at her hand inside mine and squeezed my fingers gently, a little reminder that she was here and not afraid.

"Then you are going to love the library."

Chapter Eighteen
Selene

Jude had been acting strange ever since we kissed at his show. One second he looked like he would rip my clothes off with his teeth and the next moment he'd be lost in deep thought. An internal battle raged inside him, and I didn't know which side I wanted to win. I'd learned a long time ago that life was short, and we could truly die at any time so living for the now became a motto for me. However, the many of us would be blessed with the gift of aging and a normal life expectancy. Jude didn't have that luxury. He knew he would die . . . and soon. He'd stayed away from people and had accepted his fate. Except now I knew he wanted to engage more with me, flirt, let himself be a man with me, but I also saw the fear of attachment . . . the vulnerability of letting someone get close when he was doomed to leave them.

I wanted to explore "us" naturally. Maybe it would turn out to be a hot night of fun or maybe more. We only had twenty-seven days. I fully understood why there stood a war in his head, and as we walked to the library, I reached deep into myself to root out the answer of what I wanted from him, too.

"Here we are." Without warning, he lifted our joined hands and twirled me around and into the room. When my eyes adjusted to the room, I gasped.

"So many books! I could cry." It was a beautiful sight indeed, there were parlor-type sofas situated across the wood floors over elegant purple rugs and hand-carved wooden bookshelves two stories high with ladders that would roll across the walls to help reach each level. Paintings and sculptures of a different time brought a regal museum vibe to the place. A fire blazed in the giant fireplace, with a single high back chair, the only seat in the room not dusty.

"I take it that's your reading spot?" I envisioned him sitting cross-legged, with one arm resting on the large side and the other flipping the page of an interesting adventure story, his tan skin glistening from the flickers of the flames, and his hair messy from having taken a shower.

"The other seats are hard." We walked farther into the room and he gestured for me to look around. There were so many choices and so many books that hadn't been opened in ages, except for one particular genre.

"Horror. I would have surely thought that being surrounded by ghosts all the time would have made the genre seem less scary to you." I let my fingers rub against the spines of the books as I walked by, wishing I could give them the attention they deserved, but I didn't have the time nor the ability right now.

"The ghost stories make me laugh, but the others I find intriguing since it is difficult to frighten me given my life's situations. I keep searching for something that will make my heart race and get that hard feeling in the pit of my stomach. Even performing doesn't give me that sensation."

"Interesting. Maybe if you want to get your heart racing you should pick up a romance. Stirs the blood to the heart and nether regions quite easily." I didn't face him after I spoke so nonchalantly. Instead I kept walking around, looking at the paintings and the books with interest. Despite wanting to stay in here forever, I craved seeing the rest of the house more.

"I've seen the library. Now show me some other interesting sights."

Jude leaned against the back of a sofa with his legs crossed casually. He reminded me of a dark-haired, tan version of James Dean.

"I've got an interesting sight for ya." He smirked and I rolled my eye. I did set myself up for that one.

"Let's go, smart-ass, I do plan on sleeping at some point tonight and you've got a big-ass house." I walked toward the door and Jude followed silently behind me. Once we exited the library, I peered in both directions and decided to head straight instead of the way we had come in or to the unknown left, where sounds of pots banging filled the air. There were more lighting sconces on the wall, and curtains hung without windows in the hallway. A candelabra with three candles flickered, and though the sight appeared eerie and scary, I had the power to also see the shimmering blue ghost holding onto it. It was a young boy who watched me with a wide grin. He obviously didn't know I could see him, so for the sake of child's joy, I feigned fear.

"Jude, how is that candelabra moving?" I leaped against Jude's body and pointed toward the boy who giggled, making the candles shake with the movement.

"I did warn you this house was haunted." Jude played along, his arms wrapping around me, protecting me from the harmless ghost before us. What started out as fun changed as soon as my body registered the hard, muscular form flushed against my back. It had been too long, and his touch made me tingle and shiver with the caress of death lingering inside him.

"You promise to protect me, right?" I whispered, my head falling back against his shoulder as my arms gripped the material of his pants beside my thighs. The boy laughed harder, enjoying his little prank as he stood ten feet away and moved the candles around slowly.

"With these very hands." His thick voice tickled against my ear, making my body squirm in his arms. His lips pressed against my hair and the boy stopped giggling.

"Eww, he kissed her." The child's face scrunched up and he ran in the opposite direction, unlike me, who wanted Jude to keep doing the offensive act on my body.

"Beautiful performance. You should have been an actress instead of a journalist." His lips moved down my neck and nipped where my shirt and skin met. His touch drove me crazy, and all of my thoughts deserted me.

"I like figuring out the secrets of people who don't want them uncovered. I like puzzles and being an actress is fake. I don't want to waste my time being someone else when I can be me, as sad and lonely as I am."

My body froze, as did Jude's. I didn't mean to say all that. If the man's lips hadn't been consuming me, I would have said something else. Instead, I admitted to this sexy man that I was sad and lonely. Fuck, was I a mess.

"Can we just forget I said all that?" I untangled myself from his arms, and walked down the hall, hoping there weren't any mirrors to show the blush of my cheeks, revealing my embarrassment.

"This way." Jude coughed and pointed toward the right that led to a set of stairs going down. He didn't say anything else, and I hoped, for now, he let it go.

Jude led the way, not looking at me as we descended the stairs into a darker hallway. There were no shimmers of ghosts hanging around, but I felt an off sensation creep up my spine. Not one of fear, but connection. A great power rested down here. My hand reached out to touch the walls, curious if I would feel it move with an inhale or exhale. Whatever pulsed with vitality, it flowed life like a human but felt deadly. It hummed in my mind, a song of comfort, and a painless death.

Jude stopped before a door and grabbed onto a candle, then a match to light the wick.

"This house was built on a natural power source . . . wild magic. Not like the power that came from the gods of ancient Greece but made up of all the energy from the Earth. The gates that hold back the dead rests here. That's the power you feel. It probably calls to you, singing to you to about death. It wants to be opened. The souls on the other side want that, but only I can unlock it. So it's wasting its time on you!" He yelled the last part to the door down the hall. I didn't want to dwell on thinking about the other side of the door holding a giant gate to hell where dead people banged constantly to be released.

"I have someone I want you to meet. Selene, this is Madam Tully."

Chapter Nineteen
Selene

"The light shines in her soul tonight. Prince, please wait outside this site." The woman with straight hair and a plump body wrapped in a flowing purple dress floated over to Jude to grab the candle, then nudged him out. My gaze darted to his, waiting to see if this was supposed to happen but he nodded and then walked back out the door. She closed the only way out and turned around to look at me.

"You know I can see you?" She didn't seemed surprised at all that Jude brought me here or that I could see her.

"Of course I know that, child. And now that he's gone, we girls can chat without all that testosterone mucking up my place. You've got that man so tied up in knots he doesn't even know what to do with himself. Oh, child, you are beautiful." The woman rushed over to me. Her cold touch caressed my cheek, then her fingers lifted some of my hair like she hadn't touched hair in a long time.

"You don't talk in rhymes all the time?" I felt awkward and wanted to get a space between us.

"No, child, I only do that to annoy Jude. He's always so uptight. Forgotten how to have a good time." She ushered me to a recently cleaned section on a sofa, then plopped down next to me. I felt out of my comfort zone, which said a lot because I dealt with ghosts all the time.

"You look just as uptight as Jude. Relax, dear. I'm not gonna hurt ya. I just wanted to talk for a bit."

I took a few deep breaths as the woman stared at me with a mischievous grin. I liked mysteries and secrets, so in a way talking to Madam Tully intrigued me. I thought about what questions I could ask like who she was, when she died, and how and what role she played in the curse, but she began answering before I uttered the words.

"I am Jude's great-great-grandmother. My husband was the fool who didn't use his gifts for their purpose and brought the curse down on us. I died of old age. Luckily the curse didn't drag me down with him. I stay because that poor boy needs me, and I am the only one who knows how to break the curse."

She reached up and twirled her hair with a frown. I wondered if she could feel the strands like she could mine or if the sensation was nothing between her ghostly fingers.

"How can the curse be broken?" If she knew, I'm sure she would have told Jude, but it was worth asking.

"He told you the rhyme to change it, correct?" She looked at my hair with longing, and my fingers went up to push it behind my ear instinctively.

"Yeah. Something about the gates sealed with thirty years blood paid and a deathly promise, and death something binds shall the curse fade. I'm still trying to figure it out. He said it was a promise to the dead that will break the curse."

Madam Tully reached over gently and put her hand over mine to stop the fidgeting I hadn't realized I'd been doing.

"He is stubborn and rooted in the idea he will die on his birthday. He never challenged his fate, never had a reason to, until now." Madam Tully released my hand and she pointed toward a deck of cards on a table. Three cards suddenly lifted from the deck and floated over. I'd seen Asher do magic, so it wasn't a shock, but it did make me curious that she had the power to do it even as a ghost.

"Wild magic works differently than your type. Even dead, I'm still full of energy and can still wield it when I want." She winked at me as the cards landed in her hand. The first one she held out for me to see in the dimmed light. I wished we had a lamp so I could see everything more clearly. Of course, no sooner had I thought it, lighters appeared around the room and candles lit instantly.

"The hanged man. Sort of ironic, but this card represents martyrdom and letting go . . . surrendering." I watched her set the card on the cushion between us, then lift the other to my sight.

"Death. Again, ironic. This card represents change. Everything must die in order to be renewed." She set that card next to the other and lifted the final card. I tried making mental notes of everything Madam Tully was telling me. It had to be important or I feel she wouldn't waste her breath to give me these warnings.

"Temperance. One of my favorite cards. It represents balance, a card of higher knowledge, and soul mates. There is eternal truth in this card." She set it down, then pushed the three of them in my direction.

"I'm assuming these cards are how to break the curse besides the riddle Jude has been given?" My finger drifted across the cards' artwork, taking in the extravagance of each detail. Like the house, even the tarot cards had style.

Madam Tully nodded and gestured for me to take them. Her hands made mine scoop them into my palm. They were delicate as expected, but for something so light a heavy weight came from accepting these cards. Three pieces to a puzzle of Jude's fate and the cursed dead.

"It's a lot to handle, child. I understand. But what I know about you, and trust me, I know a lot, is that you are strong, and despite having a hard time in the past, you believe in the power of love. You believe in not wasting this precious life that each of us are gifted." Her hand reached up to push my hair back one more time, and her fingers caressed my cheek. She lifted my chin so I would look her in the eyes.

"You fight the weight of your mind every day, and while you may let it get you down for a day or two, you always get back up and fight another day. You are the knight in this story, Selene." She smiled in a motherly fashion with pride, a smile I hadn't seen in a while. My mother loved me, and thought highly of me, but she didn't understand the struggles of depression. She didn't understand how hard it could be to feel the pure hopelessness pull you too far beyond anyone's reach. Nor did she know how difficult it was for me to drag myself out of it as often as I did. The woman before me saw that struggle. She saw what lingered beneath my skin, and it wasn't my power as a reaper. She saw the pain, the sadness that waited for the opportune moment to strike and leave me useless.

Tears I didn't know needed to be released leaked from my eyes. It was nice to be seen . . . to be truly seen, heard, and appreciated.

"Jude is very lucky to have you in his life, and as much as I hate to say it, I'm glad the curse stuck you here. I haven't met any of Jude's other family yet, but it's obvious to me who he truly admires the most if he brought me here first." I spoke through my happy tears, completely unabashed as they flowed gentle down my cheeks.

"I knew I would like you. Now as much as I want you to myself, we'll have to do it another time. You and Jude need to finish the tour and get out of here." She smiled brightly and I suspected she was pulling a "Phillip" on me and orchestrating some one-on-one time that would most likely end in fucking.

Chapter Twenty
Selene

Jude showed me the rest of the glorious house with kitchens and a ballroom that used to house beautiful parties every night in its prime. Now anything not used regularly by Jude had a thick layer of dust and cobwebs. I joked it was a miracle he didn't suffer from a respiratory problem because of the allergens coating the house. He laughed and shook his head.

As we walked, the souls around us stared for a short time before they resumed their celebrations. None of the few we talked to jumped out as a killer to me either, but I needed to see them in their regular lives and not in the high from the show.

The mansion seemed to be lost in time. So much history rested within the walls, so much heartache, and so much sadness. We'd looked out to the vast cemetery from the back section of the wraparound porch and I still couldn't fathom the number of ghosts there. This place was a hub for souls who could not go on. The majority didn't wallow in their predicament. Instead, they enjoyed the time they had left on Earth.

The moon shone over the many tombstones and mausoleums in the mansion's backyard. It was getting late, and I needed to get some sleep before working on my last draft for the paper tomorrow. I turned to Jude, and he guessed my thoughts before I even said them.

"Time to head home?"

"Yeah." A yawn followed my words, as we began our walk around the porch to where his car was parked.

"Rudy?" Jude took a step ahead of me toward a shimmering ghost sitting on the railing. He looked young and similar to Jude in a way. There was a heaviness on him, which would also explain why he sat out here instead of joining the rest of the joyful souls inside.

"Hey, sup man." Rudy stopped frowning, clearly putting up a front.

"You doing all right?" Jude asked.

"Yeah, I just thought with the power to touch and all tonight that she would have chosen me. But I'll be all right. You two lovebirds get out of here and do the horizontal tango, if you know what I mean." Rudy's eyebrows waggled at Jude, then he winked at me.

"I'll be back," he said in a remarkably well-done Terminator voice and jumped off the railing only to disappear before hitting the ground.

"He's a joker. Always trying to make people laugh, but I had a feeling he's been in love with Lucy for a while. Tonight confirms it." Jude's hand reached out to the small of my back and lightly nudged me forward, moving us away from where Rudy had made his dramatic exit.

"The girl from earlier?" The image of her hate-filled eyes directed at me made me shiver.

"Yeah, they usually hang out together. He does stunts to make her laugh and she likes it. But as far as I know, they never dated or hooked up. Looks like he wants out of the friend zone." Jude helped me down the stairs and clicked on the top of his key to unlock the car ahead.

"Maybe you should help him out. He's a friend and all. Isn't there some kind of bro-code for this stuff?" I bumped my shoulder against his and chuckled. I could totally see them plotting a way for Rudy and Lucy to get together. Jude could even give them the power to be human-like for the night, which was kind of weird.

"What are you laughing at?" He pulled me around so my body became flush with his. He was so hard and warm beneath his ringleader's attire.

"That you have this incredible gift that can probably control an army of the dead but instead you use it to let ghosts fuck for the night." I giggled. I know he did more than that, but this moment to tease him became too great to pass up.

"You have quite the mouth on you." He smiled while his gaze settled on my lips. My giggling died and was replaced by a consuming desire to use that mouth he spoke of on him.

"She's speechless already?" he teased softly, his lips, his breath coming closer and closer to mine.

"Just kiss me, ringleader," I told him, and he did as told without any resistance. A sigh that closely resembled a purr flowed from me into his mouth as we kissed . . . kissed some more.

"Let's get you home." He pulled back and helped me into his car. I wished I knew what he seemed to be fighting about in his head. One minute we were kissing, and the other he was back in his head. The further we drove from his home, the darker his thoughts appeared to turn. I didn't know if I should ask him if he needed to talk about, or if I should leave him alone. Every relationship I'd had—all two of them—were vastly different, and in the end we just couldn't relate. My issues were hard on me somedays, and I knew they were hard on someone who cared about me, too. My insecurities started to take over, and as we pulled up to my house, I felt confused.

"Cute house." He parked behind my old Jetta, then faced me.

"It's no giant mansion but it's paid for and I like it." Pride blossomed in my chest as I looked at my blue cottage. The shutters next to the windows were plantation-style and white. It looked like the type of home you might find on a beach or lake, not just outside Seahill.

"I love it. Bet it feels more like a home than mine does." I peered at his face and saw longing in his expression. The words to invite him in got stuck in my throat. I wanted to hold him, make him feel like people cared for him.

Hell, I cared for him. Jude wasn't a simple stranger to me. He was a friend, and more if I faced the truth of my feelings.

"Do you wanna . . ." His fingers stopped my lips from moving.

"I want to. You have no idea how badly I want to go in that house with you. But I can't. Not tonight."

"Why?" The question flew out before my mind caught up with the action. It wasn't any of my business as to why he couldn't come in, and he didn't owe me an explanation. I tried to take it back but instead of his fingers muting my words, his lips crushed my lips into silence.

"I want you. A lot. But even I can see you're different than any woman I've been with, and I don't know how to feel about that considering my fate." He spoke against my lips, and I wanted him to kiss me again.

"I don't know what to do," he admitted, kissing me one last time before his body moved back into the driver's seat completely. I didn't know, either, and it sucked. We were at a crossroads, and neither one of us knew which way to go. We still had time to turn back and not follow the path that led from friends to lovers to more. Part of me felt that ship had already sailed, and we had nothing left but to stay the course and fight for it.

"Let's not worry about it tonight. Get some sleep. I'll message you tomorrow." I leaned over to kiss him on his scruffy cheek, then got out of the car.

He waited there until I was safely inside, then for another few minutes. I'd hoped maybe he'd changed his mind and would come in, but disappointment hit me as I watched him back out of my driveway and head to his full yet lonely home.

Chapter Twenty- One
Selene

One week vanished in slow motion if anyone had been paying attention like I had been. Jude cancelled his show that was supposed to happen two days ago, claiming sickness. I'd tried to contact him, to see if he lied or truly suffered from some illness that kept him from performing, but he didn't answer.

I was worried about him, and while everyone went on with their lives, every single day of the past seven had felt like eternity waiting for Jude to let me know he was OK. I'd helped six souls move on from this world and even helped catch one of the six who thought it was a good idea to stab someone, then go to a restaurant down the street like nothing happened. Echo arrested him, and I'd helped that soul find peace before taking him onward. Life felt dull, and nothing had changed in the way it played out before . . . except for Jude.

The last time I saw him, he confessed that he felt confused, and didn't know what to do. I understood his pain, but after the week I just had without him, I realized my feelings had already gone past friends. I wanted to be near him, and I had no clue where things would lead if his fate turned out to be fact. I only had twenty days left with him before the debt to the gates keeping back the dead had to be paid. Twenty days before Jude had to die and end that stupid curse.

The three tarot cards Madam Tully had given me sat on my coffee table next to a half of a cup of tea. I'd researched the meaning of them and researched what they could mean besides the obvious. There had to be something more to them, some clue that I missed.

Feeling frustrated all around, I grabbed my coat and decided to take a walk in the crisp fall air. I needed to step away from those cards and think about another topic that didn't start with J and end with ude.

The breeze was strong today. The forecast called for a chilly night ahead, and I thought it would be a nice night to light up the fireplace in my living room and maybe grab a book to distract myself from my wallowing thoughts.

"Excuse me, miss, could I trouble you for a moment?" A frail voice spoke from behind, so I stopped and turned only to scream instead of smile. A shimmering blue ghost stood in the setting sun's light with a gun pointed at my heart.

"This isn't happening." I spoke aloud and the ghost man smiled, his rotting teeth and sunken skin making me cringe.

"Oh, darling, it is. Now it's been a while since I felt a woman, and now that I can, I plan on making up for lost time." He reached out. His cold finger touched my skin, leaving a greasy sensation behind. The gun pressed against my chest, its metal hard against my flesh, and fear shook my body.

This wasn't right. Souls weren't allowed to do this. Something was wrong. The ghost's gaze dropped to my heaving chest, and I acted quickly, smacking the gun out of the soul's hand, then grabbed onto his torn clothes. I closed my eyes as he squirmed, trying to get free from my grip.

"This isn't possible. I'm a ghost. You can't touch me, only I can touch you! You shouldn't even see me!" He gurgled as a red light glowed from his insides.

"I'm a reaper, darling, and let me be the first to say, "Welcome to hell." My soul left my body as we went to that other realm of the afterlife, but unlike most souls I'd taken onward, this jerk wasn't going to the place of peace. Rage, pain, anguish. Those were the sensations that crept over my skin as the ghost's whole body was consumed by the dark-red light that appeared black. He disappeared, taken to wherever bad people enjoy their version of hell, as I collapsed back into my body.

As soon as I rose to my feet, I sprinted toward my house and grabbed my keys and phone. The Hero

Society had to know what happened, to be on the lookout for any other souls taking advantage of their new power. It wasn't just the ghosts of Mallory Mansion who had special benefits. It was all of them.

The drive to Jude's mansion felt longer than the twenty minutes it took. I'd called Phillip on the way and as soon as he answered all he said was, "I know," then hung up. He knew this specific future was the one happening now.

The four hitchhikers waited with their thumbs up outside the mansion's gates like before, only this time I didn't smile when seeing them. My hands shook as I pulled up to the barrier and got out as soon as I put the car in park.

"Get me through." I didn't feel like climbing over the fence. I needed to see Jude now. The one ghost with a large hat saw my expression and held out a hand. The other souls looked at their friend then the road with longing.

"Now you know why we want to leave." He bowed his head, his corpse-like skin pulled tight against his skull as I placed my hand against his skeleton fingers. My body became weightless as he used his ghostly gift that he shouldn't have to pull me through the gate. It tickled slightly; the bars coasted through me as if I was the gentle fall breeze caressing the steel. The sensation felt like when I used my own gifts to take a soul onward, only this time, it was my whole body and not just my soul that made the journey to the other side.

"Can you stop it?" the hat ghost asked and my lips tightened. I had no idea how stop it.

"I'm gonna try."

"You might die," he retorted, and I shrugged. Death didn't scare me; it never had.

"Then I'll die for a worthy cause." I waved goodbye to the ghost as he let go of my hand and I ran toward the mansion's doors.

As I ran, I thought about my life leading up to this moment, and the future I'd be thrown into once I got to the massive house at the end of the driveway. When I was a teenager, I'd willingly walked into death's embrace. I was refused and came back to live my llfe the way it had been meant to be lived, by helping others, solving crimes, and actually doing more than existing in chaos. Until now, I had been coasting through my years, scared to make the true leaps that made this life worth living. Not anymore. Fear of getting hurt and fear of rejection were only that. Fear. I thought being around dead people made me live without fear, but I was wrong.

This time when I knocked on death's door, I ran into his arms and sealed my fate against his lips.

Chapter Twenty- Two
Jude

I never thought a kiss could be both heaven and hell. A week. That's how long it had been since I'd tasted Selene's lips and savored her whimpers against my mouth. I felt like a man on the brink of starvation. I wanted more. No, I needed more. But I couldn't.

"I'm surprised to see you here." I hated pulling away from her. I wanted to touch every inch of her warm skin against mine. She looked at me with explosive desire, and the sight nearly brought me to my knees.

"I was just attacked by a soul with a gun. Something is really wrong. It's not just your mansion ghosts that have extra gifts." Her hand caressed my cheek and instinctively my head leaned against her touch. My body and soul reacted to her without hesitation, that wasn't the problem.

"Are you OK?" My fingers checked for signs of any injury along her cheeks and neck.

"I'm fine, but we can't let anyone get hurt. We have to fix this. I've already called the Hero Society but I'm not sure what they can do. What is super speed or changing into an animal or manipulating metal against a ghost." She took a step away from me and paced, while rambling about the dire situation.

I sensed her pain and frustration. I'd spent the week trying to figure out how to fix the gates to the other side without me dying in the process. Anything to stay alive past my birthday. Anything to have more time with Selene. "They can't do anything. Maybe the witch can, but that is only temporary." I sighed; my shoulders dropped from the weight of my words spoken aloud.

"We're the only ones that can see them and can actually do something." She rushed back to my side, her hands touching me, and the anger simmering beneath my skin boiled over.

"It's useless. The only thing that can stop all of this is for me to go fucking hang myself in the tower like the rest of my godforsaken family. Just leave, Selene. I'll take care of the world's ghost problem soon." I didn't care if I sounded like an ass. She needed to stay away for both of our sakes. I had been starved for her touch, and she will be heartbroken when I died. What was the point of getting attached and chasing heaven when I would be dooming us to misery?

"It's not useless. We can do something. We have to try!" Her voice raised and I walked away, refusing to fight with her. I could only handle so much of the hope in her words. I didn't have the luxury of hope.

"Jude! You fucking coward. Fight with me. Be with me."

It was the hitch in her voice when she uttered those three words that stopped me. "You'll get hurt." I wasn't an idiot, I saw where she and I were heading a week ago, and made the decision to stay away. I'd never had a reason to hate my fate of dying, until her. Now I was bitter, and resentful. . . Didn't she see it? The only outcome for us is anguish, the same pain that led my mother to leave her child behind while she followed my father into death.

"I'd rather live with hurt than having lived without being with you."

My heart ached as it thumped hard against my chest, and my head hung low. The weight of my fate was too much. I didn't know what to do anymore. I tried to stay away and had warned her. I did everything I could to fix those cursed gates to hell, but every attempt I made at changing the course of my future failed.

"Come with me." I held out my hand, and she latched onto it in seconds. Silence stayed in the air between us as we walked into the house and to the stairs leading to the basement.

We walked past Madam Tully's doo, and stood before the entrance that housed the doors.

"It may be a lot at first but just keep holding my hand. As long as you have someone to lean on, the darkness doesn't weigh so heavy." My words were cryptic but there wasn't really another way to put it. She'd see, and despite wanting to take her as far from this place as I could, my free hand reached out to open the door.

My teeth clenched as I took the first step into the dark room. My fingers gripped onto Selene's, and she gave me a little squeeze of support. This room, or portal, appeared dark until the door shut behind us, sealing in the poor souls that walked up the gates of the other side, the only thing that truly kept the dead at bay.

"Is that . . .?" Selene gasped, and her other hand gripped onto my arm.

"Yeah."

A red and golden mist began to form in the room as the walls broke apart, giving way to an endless realm. We were no longer in the basement of my mansion but standing on a dark-blue stone road, with nothing but smoke coming from the trees around the rocks we stood on. The gates were large and made of sharp onyx weaved against golden rods with pointed tops. There was no lock or chains holding them together. They were sealed with magic.

A shimmering blue hand reached through the gates, then pulled back immediately as if burned, which is what a ghost did when trying to get through the gate.

"They're trying to get through." She took a step closer, her fingers gripping me tightly.

"There are more on the other side than there were a few months ago. It's like they know the gates are failing. I don't know how or why it's happening, but the ghosts are making a mass exodus here." Selene pressed further against me, her body shivering from either the chill or fear.

"Do you know what is happening?" she asked, and I pointed to one of the golden rods that appeared more of a reddish brown than gold.

"The gates are breaking. Literally. A chink in the magic. I've tried to seal it back, including feeding it my blood, but nothing has worked." I pulled back my sleeve and showed her the cut made across the tanned skin of my forearm.

"Jude." Her whisper of my name made me close my eyes. I wanted to hear my name coming from her lips for a long time.

"I need to get out of here. I'm having trouble fighting back some depressing thoughts."

I nodded and turned us to go.

"No!" a man screamed from behind us. A ghost crawled through the broken section of the gate. His fingernails dug into the sapphire-blue rocks.

Anger bubbled up from my chest as I pulled Selene close, covering her eyes. I held my other hand out to use my death magic.

"Go the fuck back to hell," I growled, and watched as a dark smoke curled around the ghost, wrapping around his fingers one by one, up his arm, then hook his neck. I gripped my fingers tightly, and the ghost screamed while my power pulled him back through the burning gates.

I needed to leave more of my tendrils of darkness behind to guard the broken area or more would be escaping. No one else had the power I did to relieve me when I grew tired, and I needed breaks.

"Let's go." I walked with Selene in my arms out the door and slammed it so hard, the walls rattled beside it.

Chapter Twenty- Three
Selene

He didn't want me to see his power wrap around the ghost like a dark noose to drag it back to the other side. Maybe a normal person would fear his power, but I wasn't normal or afraid of him.

Jude walked us back upstairs silently, while I counted my blessings. Being in that room had brought out all my horrifying moments of depression, and it made me feel small and alone. My hand gripped Jude's hand tightly.

"Come home with me," I blurted out as we neared the doorway for me to leave. I wasn't giving up on this. I'd made that decision as soon as I saw his face when he opened the door. Whatever force pulled us together was too strong, and I didn't care.

"Selene." His voice was thick with the pain of denying us.

"As long as you have someone to lean on, the darkness doesn't feel so heavy. That's what you said. So lean on me, Jude. Let me be the one to hold your hand and follow you into the dark." I lifted our joined hands up to my lips and pressed a kiss to his warm skin. His lips parted, as his eyes darted to my lips, then up to my eyes wistfully.

"Just tell the Hero Society to meet here tomorrow morning. 9:00 a.m. I'll see you then, Selene." He gently used his other hand to unwind our joined connection, then took a step back, giving me his answer.

He was afraid. Instead of flinging hurtful words at him, I nodded once and left. I'd made my case, and the ball sat waiting in his court. He had to decide what he wanted and what he deemed worth enough to damn everything else. The chilled wind bit against my face as I cried unexpected tears. The pain increased as the gates opened for me this time as I exited the Mallory property. Jude must have been watching me leave. He wasn't going to run out of his house to tell me that we'd walk hand in hand in the darkness. He'd rather shoulder his burden alone. I could yell and scream at him all I wanted, but the choice had to be mutual.

The hitchhikers were gone as I walked to my car and started it up. The silent drive grew heavy on my emotions all the way back to my apartment. As soon as I got inside my warm home, I lit a fire in the hearth and called Phillip.

"What's shaking?" he answered, while a police siren wailed in the background.

"Hey, is everything OK over there?" I thought about getting back in my car and rushing to help but there most likely wouldn't be anything I could do unless someone died. I didn't have super strength or speed like Leo or spy skills like Lilith. I talked to the dead and took them to the afterlife, not exactly save the day material.

"A robber knocked over a candle at the hippie shop. He thought there would be pot there, but he was wrong. All is good here. What's going on with you?" I heard the curiosity in Phillip's voice, maybe wondering what words I would say to determine the future.

"Jude wants the Hero Society to meet at his house tomorrow morning at nine. The gates to the other world are falling apart, but he has an idea and wanted to talk to everyone about it." At least that was my hope. Something needed to be done about the problem. If he didn't have an idea, then maybe one of the others would come up with one.

"Sounds good, I'll let everyone know. Gwendolyn and Arthur will stay behind. I'm pretty sure Gwendolyn would have a heart attack if she saw his place." Phillip laughed.

Gwendolyn had Asperger's and was the smartest of the group, but she was OCD and did not like messes. She was always organizing something at the Hero Society headquarters. She couldn't help herself. I know she tried hard to restrain her obsessions when she came to my cottage, but sometimes I found her reorganizing my pantry.

"Very true. Well I guess I'll let you go, then we'll meet up tomorrow." I glanced around my empty home and thought about what my next move would be. I needed to do something to get out of my head, anything to keep my depression from collapsing over me like a weighted blanket.

"Selene, are you doing OK? My turn to ask you. Everything is good here. You can talk to me." Phillip's offer made me smile. We got along really well, so when he had the time to talk, I almost always took the opportunity to do it.

"I think I'm falling for Jude, which seems crazy since we haven't known each other long, and he is destined to die in seventeen days. I tried to plead my case to him that we should enjoy the time we have, but he wouldn't budge. Everything is happening so fast. Ghosts can do real damage, the gates to the other side are falling apart, and I miss him."

My long-winded ramble silenced Phillip on his side of the phone. Only the sound of sirens echoed from the speaker.

"I put myself out there and it didn't help." I plopped onto my sofa and pulled my legs in close, wanting to curl up into myself and cry some more.

"You did the right thing, getting your feelings out. If you would have kept them in and he died without knowing you wanted him, then that regret would have haunted you longer than you realize. He is at a crossroads in his life. One way is the easy way, the other not so much. It's up to him now." If Phillip was with me, I'd give him a big hug. Despite feeling hurt and rejected, I knew I made the right choice.

"I think you need to make some tea. Start the water for the big bathtub of yours, and don't forget to check your mail. Might be something important in there to cheer you up." I heard Phillip's conspirator grin through the phone. Whatever letter or gift waiting for me was bound to make me smile.

"Alright, you doing ok?" He wasn't asked that question often, knowing all the futures made life sometimes a little easier for him but I understood the strain it caused on his mind. Constantly paying attention to the scenes playing out in his head and making difficult choices that sometimes led to people getting hurt. It wasn't an easy gift to have, but he made the most of it.

"Yeah, I'm good. Ready to get home to my girls."

"I'll let you go then and get started on those orders you gave me," I said. While tea and a bath sounded relaxing, along with a good book, it wouldn't soothe my heart completely. However, it would help for now.

I put my teapot on the stove, and then put Epsom salts and lavender essential oils in my bath water to help calm my nerves. While I waited for the bath and tea to be ready, I opened the door to get my mail, only to see Jude standing on my porch with his hand raised, ready to knock.

Chapter Twenty- Four
Jude

I knew I made a mistake as soon as I saw Selene walk past the gates to my home. My chest hurt so bad I thought I was having a heart attack. I had been ready to suffer alone, take on the weight of my morbid destiny on my own, but as I watched her walk away with her head hung low, I knew I couldn't do it. Having Selene as mine was worth the pain in the end, even if we only could be together for a short time. I'd grabbed my keys and ran to the car after staring at the road for a few minutes while I thought about how I'd make it up to her.

Seeing her now, with those wide eyes and shocked expression, every word I'd rehearsed in the car failed me.

"I missed you. Immensely." I took a step closer, daring to reach out and touch her cheek with my thumb as tears swelled against her long lashes.

"You were right. We are worth whatever hurt in the end as long as while I'm alive, I can call you mine." Selene's shoulder quivered, and those tears flowed freely down her cheeks. I hoped it meant she was overwhelmed with joy, but I was afraid I had showed up too late. I had been a dick and a coward. But I hoped she knew it wasn't easy for me to let someone else in and share the load of my destiny. I'd been avoiding this type of connection all my life, and now with only seventeen days left, I was willing to let my walls down. All for her.

I caressed her cheek and waited while she released whatever emotions she felt so she could speak to me. "Should I go?" I half-teased, as my other hand cradled her face, her glistening eyes staring at mine with something I didn't understand.

"No, you jackass. Get inside here and kiss me." She laughed and I stepped into her house and lowered my lips to hers.

The barrier between this undeniable pull between us broke, and I sure as fuck wasn't stopping it now. Her hands buried themselves in my hair, pulling me closer as her body writhed against mine. My touch moved to her breasts, to her waist, then to her ass, lifting her up against me to move somewhere more comfortable.

"Bed's that way." She pointed while her lips roamed my neck. Her hot mouth and tongue against my skin caused me to growl from a primal part of me.

"Fuck," I cursed, as I flexed my hips against hers. The need to bite, to claim, to fuck constricted all my thoughts.

"Too far." The thirty feet to her bedroom was way too far. I needed her now, against the wall, bent over her couch.

"Jude, please . . ."

I set her down, sandwiched between me and the wall close to her bedroom. Our hands frantically yanked and gripped at the clothes in our way of what we wanted. I'd thought about her body so often, and despite the desire to lick every inch of her, nibbling and leaving my marks, the need to claim was too powerful. I ripped her bra off with a snap, and her black panties were the next to go. My hand went to her sex. She moaned as my fingers found her wanting and ready. A guttural growl reverberated from my chest, as a shiver broke over my skin as her delicate hand wrapped around my cock, once it was sprung free from my denim. The kisses I had been pecking on her bare shoulder turned into a bite on the sensitive flesh, and her knees went out with a moan on her lips.

"Jude." My name on her lips was a plea, and I wouldn't be denying this woman a damn thing. Not anymore. I wasn't going to let my shitty hand at life stop me from giving Selene the best seventeen days of our lives.

Her hand left my cock, and I lifted her up, ready to slam home inside her.

"I'm clean. Trust me?" I held her body over me, waiting, wanting to hear she was OK with this before I buried myself within her heat.

"Me, too. I trust you, Jude. Please, please . . ." she murmured against my lips, and I didn't need another please from her. Without hesitation I impaled Selene on my cock. My body tensed as her teeth bit into my lip. The taste of blood tinged with the pleasure of her warm sex squeezing my cock almost made me come.

"You're my heaven." An admission that felt stronger than any declaration of love. My fingers gripped her ass as I pulled back slightly, then slammed home, over and over. Her tits bounced and I was torn between watching her hooded eyes on me and my body as I lifted her up and down or watching my dick as it slid into her pussy, disappearing like a new magic trick. My favorite magic trick.

"You are my Jude. I don't need heaven. Just you." She groaned as her hands went to my face and pulled me closer to connect our lips, her body flushed against mine, every thrust became slower and harder. I'd never felt this level of intimacy before. Her words sliced me open, and my heart beat solely for her. With her wrapped around me, I felt forged anew, and I would fight for this . . . for us. Selene was worth everything, even if I had to raise an army of the dead to take on the world.

Tendrils of my power broke free and curled around her like a dark smoke.

"Oh yes!" she cried out, as my tendrils of death caressed her skin. Being near death had euphoric sensations for her, and when she kissed me, it was like she kissed death.

Death ran in my veins, and only she could handle that from me. I flexed my power more, sending a flare of its strength into her house. The pulse of it hit her as I fucked her harder. She screamed and her pussy clamped down on me as her release hit. Every muscle in my body tensed from the sudden sensation and I came with a roar that shook the wall behind her writhing body.

Our breathing echoed around the hall as I lowered us to the floor, her body tangled around mine like an octopus.

"I . . ." She couldn't form words, and I knew the feeling.

"Yeah." After a few minutes of recovery, I'd be lunging for her body again.

"I've never had anything like . . . Wait. Why is my leg wet?"

I felt something wet touch my ass.

"Oh my God! I forgot to turn off the bath water!" She rose off my cock and scrambled for the bath that had overflowed into the hallway, soaking her floors and us.

Chapter Twenty- Five
Selene

"Oh that feels so good." I moaned at the bliss being massaged into my body.

"Don't do that, or you're going to make me attack you again," Jude warned as he massaged my foot in the tub. After I'd turned off the water, I grabbed some towels to clean up the mess that had spread into my hallway. Jude saw me bent over with my ass in the air and couldn't help himself. Apparently, my ass called to him.

My water bill was going to be high for this month so once we were done with round two of mind-blowing orgasms we decided to soak in the bath together. It was the right cozy temperature and we fit OK for a tub with two people in it.

"What do you dream of, Selene?" We'd been asking each other questions for the past ten minutes, trying to learn everything there was to know about the other. The way his eyes lit up and how he smiled was nice. He cared what I said and he was easy to talk to. I liked it.

"I don't have big dreams. Maybe that would be appalling to some people, but I just want to live a happy life. Be around people who get me, smile, help those in need as best as I can. What about you?" As soon as I asked, I wanted to take back those words. Jude didn't let himself dream, not with his looming death. His head dipped, and he focused on his masterful fingers on the arch of my foot.

"When I was younger, when I thought I still had a chance of living past thirty, I wanted to get married, have a pet, and do something meaningful. All the other bullshit made me feel joy for a short time, like skydiving and traveling. I did all that because when you know you are gonna die, you try to knock stuff off your bucket list, but you tend to stay away from the deep stuff. You know?"

I understood him, but I felt the opposite after my own experience with death. Life was short whether you knew when it would end or not. You had to live and do what you wanted now, even experience heartbreak from falling in love.

"I'll marry you." Jude's fingers stilled and his head flew up instantly upon hearing my three little words.

"Jesus, Selene, you don't waste time." He laughed and shook his head.

"It's your dream, and you only have this life. Why would you not do something that you truly want?"

I would marry him, not because of pity but because I enjoyed him. I missed him like hell in the week we didn't talk. His presence gave me a peace I never knew before, not to mention the amazing things he does with his body to mine. One life. That's it.

"You don't want that." He couldn't wrap his head around the idea that I was telling the truth, which was fine, I guess some people wouldn't leap that quickly.

"I do, but that's OK. I'm fine just being with you." I pulled my foot from his slack grip and maneuvered my lips toward his. We needed a distraction from the thoughts of his death and I could think of a few things that would empty my mind quickly.

"Siren," he murmured as my lips pressed against his, my thighs straddling his hips as his growing cock bobbed up to meet my core.

"I'm not the kind of siren that will lure you to your death, I'm the kind that lures you away from it." I tried to give hopeful thoughts, as I kissed my way down his neck, and then to his wet chest.

"If you're the last thing I feel when I die, I'll die a happy man." He groaned as I bit lightly against his nipple.

"No dying. No more talk of dying. Jude, we're gonna figure this out, and then you are gonna bang me on the hood of your sexy car the day after your birthday. Do you understand?" I sat up and rubbed my core against his considerable length, teasing him.

"Yeah, I do." His hands kneaded my breasts and I positioned him beneath me, then sank down slowly.

Sex with Jude was unexplainable. Maybe it was stupid to fall for him, especially if I couldn't deliver on saving him, but I wouldn't stop until I exhausted every option to make sure this curse broke before his death.

"If you're thinking in there, then I'm not doing a good job." Jude kissed my lips, the scab from my bite earlier tickling the sensitive flesh and I smiled.

"Thinking of you now."

"Never stop." He lifted us up and out of the water, then walked to the bedroom.

For hours we explored each other's bodies and souls. By the time we fell asleep, I knew Jude's heart and character, and I wanted to protect him. He had so much to give this world, and I hated that he'd hid himself from it for the vast majority of his life. His power, his shows, hell his smile could make life better for many people.

He held me close, his arms curled around my torso like his favorite teddy bear as he slept peacefully. I wished I could have said the same. I slept, but as the light began pouring through the window, I laid there in his grasp, thinking about what could be done.

I tried to live in the moment, but my brain wouldn't shut off as the journalist in me came out to play. I had been presented with a curse, a challenge even, and now the stakes were someone I loved. I needed to solve the puzzle and save him, along with the world.

"Do we have to get up?" Jude's husky voice broke through my thoughts and I smiled. He sounded sweet and youthful, like the weight on his shoulders didn't feel too heavy. I hoped I helped take some of the load off of him.

"Someone wanted to have a meeting with the Hero Society early in the morning. I didn't make the rules." I giggled and his fingers explored my naked body.

"Someone didn't know they'd be fucking all night and have the opportunity to continue in said morning." He pressed kisses to the back of my neck and I realized I enjoyed waking up with a sweet, sleepy Jude.

"Someone should have been more optimistic." I wiggled against his body behind me and felt him grow with every wiggle. Oh yeah, I definitely enjoyed waking up with Jude in my bed.

"I'll show you optimistic." He pressed his length against my ass and all thoughts that plagued me moments before disappeared.

Chapter Twenty- Six
Selene

"It smells like dead people in here." Echo's nose scrunched up on her face, with Asher laughing at his woman's expression.

"There are dead people here. Be nice, kitten." The warlock teased her as he wrapped his arms around her body and kissed her cheek. I always liked them; Asher's magic came from the wild magic of the Earth, probably the same as Madam Tully. Echo and Asher both wore matching leather jackets and jeans with boots. It was cute that they always looked like a couple even without trying.

We sat in the parlor room of Jude's mansion with a burning blaze heating up the room in the massive fireplace. Everyone from the Hero Society sat comfortably on the couches, ready for Jude to discuss whatever he called the meeting to speak about.

"We should have a party here." Lilith smiled and danced around the room like a ballroom dancer. Leon shook his head and plopped on the sofa next to Asher. Lilith continued to dance to the music in her head, but I knew she would be listening to everything in the room.

"Feels weird here." Rose added her opinion to the mansion and Draco wrapped his arms around her, bringing her body against his torso. Esme and Dorian sat on the sofa I was snuggled into while trying not to glance at them more than normal. Dorian was the only demigod left in the world. His presence here on our side was a big deal.

"Thank you guys for coming." Jude stood by the fire, his pensive stare touched on every one of our faces, lingering on mine for more than a few seconds before addressing the group again.

"I'm sure Phillip has updated you. The gates to the other side are deteriorating. I'm not sure on the numbers but there are ghosts that have powers they shouldn't. They are able to show themselves and touch things and people, then disappear. It's dangerous, and people have already died at my show because of it."

"Shouldn't we be worried about ghosts hearing us right now?" Echo paced behind the couch while looking around, sniffing.

"No. I used my power to kick them out of the house. We can speak freely here." Jude shoved his hands in his pockets to hide his nervousness. On the outside he looked completely calm, at peace even, but I knew underneath he didn't feel comfortable. I understood his emotions. It was something we both had in common.

"So, what do we do about this?" Draco asked, his fingers lazily caressing Rose's hand as he asked.

"I don't know. None of your gifts are a match against the dead. I had hoped with you all here, we could discuss a plan of action." Jude glanced at me, and I rushed to his side. The need to touch, to feel his skin against mine was unfathomable.

"Not sure what any of us can do against ghosts," Dorian agreed, and the rest of us sat in silence while we thought about what we could do together. My hand squeezed Jude's as he kissed my cheek.

"There's a lot of magic here. We could tap into it and put a temporary bind on the break in the gates. It should stop anyone from escaping and stop it from spreading any further." Asher offered up his idea, which sounded good to me, but I'm sure there would be a catch.

"How about we raise an army of the dead to battle the dead?" Lilith's melodic voice rang around the room, and everybody tensed.

"I don't think that's a good idea." Rose wrinkled her nose, and Jude's body trembled beside me as his face paled.

"Could you do that?" I whispered, my curiosity wondering if he held that much power inside him. His lips tightened into a thin line as he nodded. Holy shit, he could raise an army of dead people. A tendril of death's darkness leaked from Jude and curled around our joined hands. My body shuddered, but not from a chill or fear. I was drawn to Jude in a way that should scare me, being with him, it was immense and endless. I didn't run from his dark power. I leaned into it, like a purring cat against its master.

"Anymore clues as to who is the murderer of your show?" Echo asked Jude, and he shook his head. I'd managed to talk to a few of the ghosts before the Hero Crew arrived, and I had my suspicion as to who the killer was but I needed more evidence before I made my thoughts known.

"We need to find that ghost. Put a band-aid on the gates if we can. Do we know how to repair it permanently, and fix this whole mess?" Phillip asked.

I rubbed my thumb against Jude's hand tenderly.

"I have to die on Halloween, and everything will be fixed." Jude stood tall, confident even, but I sensed the power beneath him pulse with fear.

"Is there a way we can do it that doesn't involve you dying?" Esme spoke for the first time, and I watched as her fingers drifted toward the golden vein of her power on her arm. She had the gift of healing, but every time she used it, she grew closer to her own death.

"The gates sealed with thirty years blood paid, a deathly promise be made, until death do you bind shall the curse fade. That's what my witch who knows the future said. She promises that the Mallory curse will end with me. My ghosts and I made a deal that they will give me one hell of a last year with the performances and then I'll take them with me. A deathly promise."

When he said it like that, a little warning ran in my thoughts. His words didn't sound right. There was something more to the saying, something we hadn't thought of or were blind to, like those three cards Madam Tully gave me. I needed more information.

"Interesting. I still vote we find a way for you to not die. You're one of us now." Lilith stopped dancing and casually sat on Leon's lap.

"I didn't say I was —" Jude started to speak.

"Welcome to the hero family, Jude. We are so honored to have you! We'll send the welcome packet in the mail soon." Lilith clapped and everyone smiled at her theatrics.

"I'd just go with it." I leaned in and whispered against his neck, then he shook his head slightly.

"Can we interview the ghosts today, maybe find out some history of your performers?" Echo was ready to get on with the investigation and so was I.

The answers to preventing his death were right in front of me. I needed to find them.

"I'd like to talk with your witch, if that's OK." Asher stood. One of us would have to go with him to Madam Tully, and the other would have to help Echo with the interrogations since we were the only two in the room who could communicate with the dead.

"Yeah, she'd enjoy some company. Selene, you take Asher, and I'll start bringing in some of my performers. If anyone doesn't want to stay, I think this meeting can be over. We will try to bind the gates and keep what is happening in Seahill from reaching the rest of the world. Asher and Madam Tully might be able to come up with a way for you all to fight back a ghost, but we'll see. Let's monitor the situation, and hopefully we can fix it before it gets out of hand." Jude talked to them like a leader, and they all responded with nods of agreement to his words.

"Let's go talk to some dead folks." I smiled and untangled my hand from Jude's, ready to get the truth and help solve this case.

Chapter Twenty- Seven
Selene

I stared at my notes from the interrogations, and Madam Tully's discussion with Asher that covered my dining table. Echo, Jude, Asher, Rose, Draco, and I talked to the performers until the sun crested over the graveyard behind the mansion. History. So much history weaved between the crew and Jude's family. These people had been stuck there for so long, I wouldn't be surprised to find out many of them were killing people for the sport of something to do. A little fun in their boring lives.

The muscles around my eyes ached from focusing intently on the handwriting before me. Some of the souls were good, just people caught in a tragic story, while others weren't always on the right side of the moral border when they were alive. Ghosts loved to gossip. Lucy was the circus slut. She slept with everyone she could and tempted young men into leaving their families to join her on the road, only to move on to the next guy she found interesting. A fight starter, one of the trapeze artists called her, while giving me all the juicy details about each performer.

The little boy who had tried to spook me with the candelabra had been abandoned on the road, so he was given the job of caretaker over the baby elephant. He was eight years old and named Caleb. His pet he'd given the name of Titan. Everyone helped raised him the two years before the incident with Jude's great-great-grandfather. The elephant chose to stay with his friend, instead of moving on to wherever animals go. It was the same for the tiger, who belonged to a woman named Joselyn, who was married to the original ringleader. He'd left before the curse took everyone down with them. He thought that performing for the rich folk at the mansion was beneath their talents. According to Joselyn, he not only left them before the show, but ran off with the future-telling gypsy. Maybe the gypsy had known what would happen, or maybe they just wanted a life together away from the circus.

Joselyn took over from then and never performed. She kept everyone in line. Draco spoke with her, through me, and decided they were similar in personality. Therefore she wasn't the killer. I believed him. She seemed tired of being in the state of waiting. All she wanted was to move on. Most of them wanted that. Staying on Earth after death sounded fun at first, especially those who feared death, but after a few years of not truly living, dying got old.

Rudy, the friend who had been upset about Lucy not choosing him for a bedmate, was a character. He'd been a floater in the circus before, the type of man who could do anything. His bright smile lit up the room, and his charismatic personality drew everyone toward him naturally. But I could see his issue with Lucy causing a rift in the group. He was stuck in the friend zone, forever longing to be more in her eyes. While he wasn't my top suspect, I couldn't cross his name off my list. He had an underlying monster hiding behind that smile. Rose confirmed it to be jealousy. Jealous of what, though? Could have been the love he saw between Rose and Draco or that Echo turned into a viper to see if she could pick up a different heat signature than a warm-bodied person.

Listening to Madam Tully and Asher gave me a headache. They talked about a binding spell for the gate. Both seemed confident it could work. Although it would be a temporary fix, it could give us the time to break the curse and restore the balance between the living and the dead. However, she didn't give me any more hints as to how I could help Jude with his fate.

"You already have the truth. It's all within you." She pulled me into a tight embrace before telling us to go join the others.

It had been hours since I had left the mansion, and all I'd managed to decipher from the mess on my table was that I was in way over my head. My focus drifted toward the three cards I'd placed near Madam Tully's notes. I wished I understood the secrets they held for the situation at hand. The clock continued to tick while we searched frantically for a way to end the curse and find a killer. Halloween was in one week and then time would be up. I'd spent nearly every night with Jude, and my days working on ferreting out the truth of his world. He'd had a show go on without someone dying, which made his success grow further. I loved seeing his smiling face from the crowd's applause. He lived for entertaining the masses and he was very good at it. But despite the cease of murders at his show, unexplained crimes in Seahill had skyrocketed. The Hero Society tried their best to contain the souls, but they didn't have the right gifts to really deal with a ghost.

A welcomed knock on my door gave me the excuse to walk away from my notes. I needed a breather, and talking to someone else would be nice for a change. Jude was supposed to be dropping by soon, so I opened the door without even looking to see who stood on the other side. I should have thought about that decision more methodically.

Hands clamped over my mouth as an arm banded around my waist, pulling me into my home as I thrashed for my life.

"I'm gonna take my hand off you, and you're not gonna scream. Understood?"

The hand disappeared and I whirled around to see Rudy standing in my living room, the faint shimmering of his ghostly soul bouncing off my pale green walls.

"How the hell are you here? Why are you here?" The barely contained anger in my voice made Rudy's expression tense, but he held his ground.

"Only a few more days until the curse is over, and its power over us is fading. I came to warn you. Some of the others are plotting to hurt you and your friends. They think Jude is going to go back on his word with us because he has you now." He reached out to gently caress my cheek, and I smacked his hand away. He smiled from the sensation of my touch. An eerie awareness slid down my spine, but I bit back the disgust riled in my belly.

"Thanks for the update. Any way I could get you to tell me who exactly is after me and my friends?" Despite the gossip and how the crew fought with each other, they were very tight-knit group, more like a family.

"I can't but I just want you to watch out. Jude really cares for you, and I'd hate to see anything come between that." His voice switched into a different accent with ease.

"Thanks." This whole discussion made me wary.

"For what it's worth, I hope he gets what he wants with you. Maybe you guys will get married soon. At least one of us will get the girl." He winked, while his hand lifted and a single finger pointed toward my nose and tapped it lightly. He disappeared like . . . well . . . a ghost.

By the time Jude arrived, I hadn't moved. "Hey, Selene, you left your door open—" If he was going to say anything else, the words were lost as soon as he saw me trembling.

"I sense death here. What happened?" Jude's armed surrounded me, and I crumpled against him.

Chapter Twenty- Eight
Jude

I understood Rudy's wild actions, but he shouldn't have done them. He should have fucking talked to me. As soon as Selene collapsed in my arms, I carried her to the couch where she sobbed and told me what happened between them.

Some of the performers were plotting against her and the Hero Society? I'd have some big words to say about that when I got back to the mansion. I'd bind their asses to the floor with my power until the curse took us all. I didn't give a fuck. One threat against my woman's life was one too many.

He scared her when he grabbed her, and even though she deals with dead people daily with her gift, they've never come into her house or touched her.

My fists throbbed with the need to smash something, to bang on my chest, and protect my Selene from any threat.

Every thought in my head told me to race back to the mansion and do something, but I couldn't leave Selene like this. We needed to live in this moment, to feel the love we shared with every breath we shared.

I knew she loved me. I may be shit with the emotions of the living but I could decipher love when I saw it. My mother loved my father so much it destroyed her, but in death they still had each other. They had looked at one another like they were the only light in their dark lives. Madam Tully looks at me with a different kind of love, the type a mother would give to her son. Since my parents were so absorbed in themselves most of the time, Madam Tully was more of a parent than they ever were to me.

My heart thumped harder. Selene had no idea how open she was to those around her. It was like gazing into her bright soul with every glance I could steal. "Let's go lay down." I stood with her cradled in my arms and walked us to her cozy bed. It wasn't as big as mine or as elegantly decorated, but I loved it anyway. I loved her home, and how warm it felt. My mansion was cold and dead like the inhabitants floating around in it.

"Will you stay with me?" She'd stopped crying a few minutes ago, upset at herself for displaying her emotions.

"Of course." I kicked off my shoes and laid down in the bed with her still in my embrace. She didn't need to apologize for her emotions. They weren't going to chase me away. It was a healthy response to what had happened. Her head rested against my chest as we snuggled on top of the blue comforter, my fingers moving up the side of her body to gently massage her scalp.

"I'm afraid," she whispered, so quietly her voice almost blended with the chilling wind outside the window.

"You don't need to be afraid of Rudy or any of the performers. I'll take care of— "

"I'm not afraid of your crew or Rudy. I mean it wasn't fun what Rudy did but if the curse is fading, then I could probably deport all their asses to hell if I wanted to. My body screams for me to do my job around them. So it wouldn't bother me. I'm afraid to lose you."

A lump settled in my throat, blocking the words to ease her worrying mind. I couldn't truly promise anything. Time wasn't on our side, and this pain of her kiss trembling against my cheek made everything worse. I had feared this moment all of my life.

"It's not over yet," I murmured, as I shifted my body to kiss her. We didn't have much time, and even though I hated that I'd be leaving Selene behind with a broken heart, I wouldn't give up these last few days living with her as mine, loving her.

"I love you, Jude." She breathed those precious words against my lips and my heart swelled so much it hurt in my chest.

"It's OK if you don't love me, and I know it seems crazy because it's so soon, but I've always known that tomorrow isn't promised for anyone. I refuse to live in regret because I didn't tell you how I felt."

My brave Selene. She didn't know the effects she had on me. I'd been ready to die months ago, wishing I could speed up the curse's deadline and get it over with. Now, she made me want to live, not just exist. She gave me courage, and with her I had something I never thought I needed.

"I love you, Selene. You are my heaven in a life of hell."

"We'll figure it out. Then on November first, we'll do something crazy to celebrate." She smiled and sealed her lips against mine again and again.

Slowly, almost painfully slow, our clothes began to disappear. Teeth and tongues clashed, then explored the bare flesh of one another. I'd never made love before. My thoughts of making love always drifted toward how stupid it seemed. Sex was sex. Only when you did it with someone you truly cared for, it was something entirely different. I worshipped Selene with my body, giving her all my strength, my power, and my heart. Moans of never letting go became our soundtrack, and I'd forever keep the blissful sound on repeat.

The scent of our sweat and sex coated the air, mingling with our panting breaths after release barreled into both of us. Moments later, Selene wiggled against my side, then fell asleep with a smile on her face. I watched her chest heave with life of every breath in her lungs. The pink tinge of her heated skin would forever be burned into my memory, for however long I had it.

The darkness of night drifted into the morning, and I hadn't slept at all. I'd been too wrapped up in my thoughts and in Selene by my side. I wanted to soak her in, imprint her in my very DNA, so even in death she would be with me.

Part of me wished that I would have met her years ago, that I could have been basking in her light before now. Only I knew that it was strange circumstances that led our fates to join as one.

"I'll be back in an hour." I kissed Selene's cheek, then rolled out of bed. She mumbled, "OK," but didn't open her eyes to see me leave her room. I would be back before she awoke, but just in case, I found spare paper among all of her notes and scribbled my message. Once the note was secure in a place she'd see, I noticed the research she'd been doing on the curse. Three tarot cards sat by Madam Tully's information. I'd seen those cards before . . . many times before.

I knew what those cards meant, and for the first moment in my life I had hope.

Chapter Twenty- Nine
Selene

The bed appeared to be cold on the side where Jude had laid when I woke up. My fingers grasped onto the pillow and pulled it close to my nose. His scent, our mingled scents from last night, lingered in the fabric. Every muscle in my body felt languid and warm. My heart radiated so much happiness I thought it would glow.

I'd had suspicions Jude loved me, but I didn't think he'd say it. Not with the fate of his death looming over our heads. His fears of leaving someone behind drove him into isolation for so long, it must have been hard for him to admit his feelings to me. The fluttering in my stomach pick up the pace. I basked in the morning light, thinking of Jude's eyes, his tan skin, and brown hair. I dreamed of a future that seemed so far out of reach but not impossible.

When the need to pee became too much to bear, I rolled out of bed and practically danced to the bathroom. After my morning routine, I settled into a pair of sweatpants and a large T-shirt. My automatic coffee pot had already began brewing, thanks to the timer ten minutes ago. I'd slept in a little later than normal, but it was welcomed after the night I'd had. Emotions had run rampant over my mind and I struggled to push them back into the depths of my head. I knew they were justified, but thanked my depression for feeling like shit for those emotions, a never-ending cycle of sadness and anger.

Just as I sat down to go over my notes and do more research on the performers, I jumped from a knock on the door. My heart raced, and my hands shook so much, my coffee spilled onto the table.

"Selene, it's Jude. Don't freak out!" Jude's voice echoed through the door and I leaped to my feet to peer through the window to make sure it was him. He stood there, bundled up in a jacket with two bags in his hands. A lightness settled in my gut, and my knees wobbled from the sight. Instantly, I unlocked the door and ushered him in.

"Shit! Your notes." Jude saw the mess from jumping up and dropped the bags on the counter. He grabbed a rag from the stove handle and rushed to the table. His actions were cute and my bright smile from earlier came back.

"Thank you." My knees were weak from the elation running through my body without abandon. He carefully wiped up the mess and set the wet papers off to the side so they wouldn't get stuck to one another as they dried. He set the rag in the sink and then stood in front of me, his hands caressing my jaw.

"Those cards. Did Madam Tully give them to you?" He sounded curious.

"Yes. Why?"

"I've had my fair share of readings with those cards. She's never let those cards leave that room as far as I know. So they must mean something big if she gave them to you." He leaned closer, his warm breath teasing my lips with the promise of a kiss.

"Yeah, she said they held the answer to breaking the curse, but I'm missing something important." I closed the distance between us, unable to take the overwhelming desire that demanded his mouth connect with mine. Our kiss heated in seconds, then as quickly as it started, Jude pulled away.

"She said the answer was in the cards?" His words had a desperate edge laced within voice.

"Yeah. Do you know something?"

His hands dropped, and he moved swiftly toward the table with me following behind him. His fingers grasped onto the first card, the hanged man.

"This card represents sacrifice, that you must release control and your fears and move forward. Kind of like 'stop resisting and go for it' card." His hand jerked as he showed me the second card.

"This card rarely means actual death. It's more a symbol of endings and transformation. Something is coming to an end to make room for better things." He quickly grabbed the next one, holding it up so I could see.

"Temperance signifies soul mates and balance. These cards prove that what we have is something that a curse can't break. I stayed up through the night with you in my arms thinking about how I wished I had more time with you. How I feared losing you and how your broken heart would shatter with my last breath. I don't feel that anymore. I feel hope." He dropped the cards back on the table and pushed my wild hair behind my ear.

"I think we need to have sex right now." I needed him inside me, claiming me, sealing those words with the hope of the love we share when we're together as one.

He smirked and grabbed my hand, bringing it down to where his growing cock pushed against his jeans.

"I wouldn't have thought this moment would warrant that, but I guess he agrees with you." I laughed and palmed his hardness through the denim.

"Claim me, mark me, and be mine forever."

His kissable lips parted. My words were those of a siren coaxing her lover into the arms of death.

Death pulled down my sweatpants and pulled up my shirt before lifting me onto the kitchen counter.

"What about your bags?"

He pushed them off the counter, and they landed on the floor with a crinkly thud.

"November first. We'll worry about the bags then."

He growled against the skin of my thighs, then began kissing, and biting his way down to my core. He wasted no time in claiming my pleasure with his tongue. One second I felt his breath against my clit, and the next he was devouring me with a savaged passion. My back arched, while his fingers joined his lips' assault on my sex, entering me with one finger pumping in and out, then stretching me with two, over and over, harder and faster as my legs began to quiver.

"Jude!" I moaned. His snarl ripped through me as I came, clenching against his fingers while his mouth sucked on that sensitive bundle of nerves above his thrusting fingers.

"You're mine forever."

His fingers were gone, only to be replaced with something bigger, much bigger.

"Yes! Yes!"

His teeth claimed my left breast as his hips pumped into my sex relentlessly. His power leaked from him like smoke, wrapping around my hands, holding me back in a way only death could. My eyes rolled back. The sensations racking my body were almost too much to bear. His lips kissed my skin gently after having given me pain, then he lifted his torso off of me. My legs were tossed over his shoulders and his hands went to my breasts, gripping toward his body with every thrust.

"Selene," he growled. My world ended and began with him. Life as I knew it shattered before my hooded eyes and cries of release bouncing off the walls.

His upper half collapsed against mine, his cock throbbing inside me as his orgasm shook him to the core.

"You make me want to live, Selene. Not just exist. Live." He kissed my neck and jaw between pants, then finally settled on my eager lips.

Chapter Thirty
Selene

"Reports show that this strange occurrence has happened at three of Seahill's cemeteries. If anyone has any information on who has been digging up graves and taking the corpses, please come forward."

I stared at the radio in Jude's car like it grew three heads. Someone broke into coffins last night and took the dead bodies?

"That doesn't sound right. Something must be going on," Jude murmured and pressed the gas pedal a little harder with his boot. We'd already driven halfway to the mansion when the breaking news drifted through the speaker. I needed to talk with some of the performers and decipher if my life and my friends' lives were truly in danger. Jude's anger grew as we neared the driveway. We were getting closer to the ghosts he grew up knowing and caring for who were now plotting behind his back.

The hitchhikers were gone as we turned onto the property. The house looked as eerie as ever, but once we stepped outside the car, we heard loud screams coming from inside. We raced toward the doors, and Jude threw them open with a loud bang. Rudy held Lucy back from one of the other performers who was mouthing off about how Lucy was a major whore. Trouble in ghostly paradise it seemed. At least Rudy found his way back to the mansion without causing chaos.

"What's going on here?" Jude bellowed, and every ghost stopped what they were doing to look at him, their mouths gaping.

"Oh, Jude, I'm so glad you're here." Lucy broke from her friend's grasp and ran to Jude with her arms wide, expecting him to embrace her when she closed the distance. Instead his hand shot out and stopped her a foot away.

"Yeah, go run to your master to get what you want. It's not enough you flirt and cause problems wherever you go but now you're trying to ruin our last chance to move on for him. You're pathetic," the ghostly woman in a tutu scoffed before disappearing.

"All right, everyone. Go find something better to do with your time right now." Jude's command left no room for rebellion and if by the looks of the performers, there were other places they would rather be than part of this mess.

"Lucy didn't start it this time. Hannah did." Rudy strutted up to Lucy's side and held his arms open for her, but she just leaned closer to Jude, completely oblivious to my presence beside him.

"I don't give a fuck. You guys have a few days until you get out of this house. You can't manage to keep your shit together until then? And you." His focus shifted to his friend with a tense jaw twitching as he glared.

"What the hell were you thinking? Why didn't you come to me?" His death power flowed out of him like ink in water. Lucy and Rudy's eyes widened at the sight, their expressions evidence that they'd never seen him truly lose the mask and hold of his gift from Hades.

"I just thought I could help. You never let me help you, so I took matters into my own hands."

"What did you do?" Lucy leveled her friend with an unnaturally beautiful scowl. He flinched as if she'd smacked him.

"I warned her that her life was in danger at her house."

"I told you that you should have stayed away." Lucy shrugged at me like the offense was no longer a big issue since it had to do with my life instead of Jude's.

"So you threaten my life? My friends' lives?" My hands balled into fists, rage seeping into my muscles, tensing to lash out on her ghostly ass.

"I've got better things to do than waste my time on plots. If I wanted you dead, I would have killed you before. I'm not one to hold grudges, unlike some people. Plus with you gone, Jude would have been in a worse mood. I wanted to sleep with him, but I like seeing him smile much more." Lucy's voice did not waver, and I felt the truth in her words. I really had thought that if anyone would have been the person to kill out of jealousy, it would have been Lucy.

"I like seeing him smile more." Rudy did a mocking impression of Lucy and all the blood in my system froze. That voice. I'd heard it before, but the face had been concealed by a hood at Jude's show.

His eyes shifted toward me, and the smile, the creepy tilting of his lips toward his cheekbones hit me like a brick to the face.

"You."

I should have seen it, should have known but I had been too caught up in the rest of the drama to miss the obvious. His talent was impersonations, and he did a very good job at them. He could have easily changed his voice to sound female, even like Lucy.

"Now that you know, I've got something to show you." Rudy gestured for us to follow him toward the living room where a modern TV sat before the old couch.

"What are you talking about?" Jude questioned him and I tugged Jude closer to me, his hands letting go of a curious Lucy who glanced back and forth between her friend and us.

Jude's eyes narrowed on my fear-stricken face, trying to piece together the puzzle I'd connected in my head.

"He's the killer," I breathed, my heart racing while I observed the room for any threats Rudy might have set up for us.

"Rudy?" Jude didn't look convinced that his closest friend would do such a thing.

"Yes, Rudy. Wake the fuck up, man," Rudy said. "You're too nice, wasting away all that talent, those looks, your life. For what? To save someone from a broken heart. You get to be alive, while I get to be stuck in the eternal friend zone with a woman you could have fucked twenty times over. You're not worthy of the life you've been given, but no worries, that'll all change soon."

And there it was. The motive behind the killings. Rudy envied Jude. Rudy wanted to live again, to be with Lucy, to party, and be free of his ghostly chains.

"You're a coward," I said, feeling a tingle in my hands that demanded I take this murderer somewhere toasty. I heard hell was particularly warm this time of year.

"Yeah, I thought about that little gift of yours and came up with a security plan to make sure I don't get taken to hell now that the curse is finicky. I plan on staying after this mess, and I don't need you two or those heroes stopping me." Rudy clicked on the TV and my heart dropped to the floor.

My friends.

Emily, with her kind heart, and the members of the Hero Society sat in a room with two ghosts and five dead corpses guarding them.

"What good is super speed or becoming an animal against a ghost who can kill? Do everything I say, and they go free. Piss me off and they die."

Oh God.

Chapter Thirty- One
Jude

Rage didn't cover the emotions flowing through my body as Rudy crowned himself king of the mansion. My pulse pounded in my veins and my fists twitched with the need to beat the shit out of my ex-friend. I wanted to tear his ghostly soul apart with my power, but I didn't know where he kept his hostages and they were defenseless against the dead.

"This is living," Rudy moaned as he walked with each of his arms slung over the shoulders of two women. Little did they know they were about to shack up with a dead man. I hated being forced to use my powers like this, for him to shack up with anyone who would spread her legs.

It was two days before Halloween, and my death day. Rudy ordered me to move the last performance to the mansion, where everyone would dress up for a masquerade to see the show and party. At the end, just before midnight, I would walk up to the tower where I had found my father dead.

Rudy had taunted me with the images of a rope around my neck for the past few days, then he'd throw in a threat of Selene dying with me to make me cooperate further. She'd been sent home, all part of the games Rudy wanted to play. He made her sit and think about what was happening to her friends, to me, while she couldn't do a damn thing. He wanted me to suffer, too, taking away the love I had found.

He had been right about me wasting my life before, so while catching up in my future, I'd stopped focusing on now. While he thought I was wallowing, I was planning a battle strategy.

Two days, one performance, and a hanging lay ahead for me, only I wasn't going down without a fight. I had something and someone to live for now and she needed me. Everyone needed me.

Screams and moans of pleasure echoed down the hall, and even Lucy who sat on the chair across from me rolled her eyes.

"He's really taking this whole living thing to the edge, huh. Gross."

I nodded, then stood to stretch, having sat for hours.

"You're leaving?" She arched an eyebrow, and I shook my head. I wasn't allowed to leave. Instead I thought I'd take a walk down to the cemetery.

"You can come if you want, but you'd have to be quiet about all you hear," I warned, and she nodded. She was as a prisoner in the house, too. Rudy loved her, and still she refused him. According to her and Joslyn, Rudy had killed before. It was why he ran away to the circus; it'd always been a stain on his soul.

We walked to the cemetery with corpses I'd never seen before guarding us with old weapons from another era. Rudy had found a way around the binding of the gates and had freed ghosts to take over their old bodies again. So the graves that had been broken into had actually been broken out of, then they all came here. I wished I knew Rudy's grand plan, but by the number of ghosts and corpses that did not belong on his property hanging around, I assumed he craved domination. After I was gone, there would be no one to fight off the dead. I had no offspring, and if Selene was allowed to live, she could only take one soul back at a time. There were at least fifty squatting on the property with a stench that could drop you to the ground, with more on the way.

"Oh, son, thank god you're OK. What is happening?" My mother floated over to me and wrapped her arms around me tightly. I gave her the power to feel, as I wished to feel her embrace again.

"Rudy's taken over, running the shots." I shrugged, while my parents gasped and jaws dropped to the floor . . . literally.

"Can't you do something about that? I know the power in you is strong enough," my dad reprimanded, assuming I had let this happen.

"He grabbed me by the heart," I admitted and a soft female hand touched my shoulder in comfort. Lucy's sad smile was directed toward me.

"You fell in love. I thought you said you wouldn't. That this curse of our family would end with you." My father's disappointed voice felt like a vice around my chest.

A tightness grew in my throat, while my jaw hardened to the point I felt my teeth could shatter. My parents just expected me to die like they had. They never wanted me to live or fight the curse. I know she didn't mean her words to be a barb but instead of being happy that I'd gotten to experience love, they wanted me to hurry up and die to end their prolonging to the afterlife.

"Not something you can control, though I tried. Sorry to disappoint." I shouldn't have come here. Being around them only made me feel shittier about the situation and emphasized how little control I had in this world.

"That's not what we meant, son. We're happy you found love before it all comes to an end. We just didn't want you to go through what we did." My mother reached her shimmering blue hand out to touch my cheek, a loving gesture from someone who hadn't loved me like a mother should.

I wanted to consult with Madam Tully and find hope in her words that something could be done.

Rudy wouldn't let me near her room, though. It was guarded with a ghost who could stab me without hesitation. Such great power to control the dead flowed through my being, but I still couldn't walk through walls.

"Right. I'm gonna go walk around while I have the blood pumping in my veins to do so." It was an asshole thing to say to them, but I didn't feel like being civil.

I said hello to the ghosts that waved at me. My grandfather was in a duel with a pirate as I passed by his tombstone, which elevated my mood. Lucy followed me around as I weaved through the mausoleums and worn-down statues in silence. She rarely came out here, since most of the performers didn't like the graveyard. Perhaps it was because of the familiar soul who always stayed by his giant crypt, sulking in the memories of what he'd done to those he cared for.

Despite being a ghost, I noticed Lucy's hands trembling as we walked past the main section of the cemetery to a quiet and less crowded area. Only one mausoleum stood beside a tall tree with moss hanging from its branches. Magically lit torches stayed fiery throughout the years and a man sat on the steps outside.

"Hello, George."

The depressed gaze of my great- great- grandfather, the man who had brought the curse upon our family looked up.

Chapter Thirty- Two
Selene

Numb and cold, I didn't cry. I was past that. Instead I endured two of the worst feelings a person could have . . . hopelessness and loneliness. Besides my parents, who as far as I knew were having a great time in Europe, I didn't know where to find my friends. No calls to Phillip to ask him what I should do or to Emily, who always made me feel a little lighter when the darkness tried to take over.

I couldn't focus on a simple thought. I drowned in the pain of losing everyone. Who was I to fight the dead? I was no one. As soon as I got home, via Jude's car that Rudy demanded I take, I collapsed on the bed and had barely moved since. Life constricted my chest, and I couldn't find the strength to get up.

I didn't even know what to do if I could get up. Who could I turn to for help? I was alone.

Alone.

The insanity that overtook me as a teenager crashed on over me, and I feared what I might do if I let it win. So I slept for hours. For a full day, trying not to give in to the siren of death beckoning me once again.

Jude's scent clung to my sheets. I breathed it in, over and over. I concentrated on each inhale and exhale, one second at a time. Anything further than that was too much to think about.

The morning before Halloween, my sadness turned to anger. My fists ached to punch something. My power urged me to be released and lash out. I wanted to, but I knew what I endured wasn't good and wouldn't truly help me in the end. I had nothing. How does a person rise from the floor when they have nothing?

"That's not true," I whispered to the empty room.

The lie caught me by surprise, and I found the strength to pull the Jude-scented sheets off my head. Light hit my eyes, and I squinted from the brightness.

I had light in my life.

I could see.

I could walk.

I had fresh autumn air to breath.

I was safe, even if safe was temporary.

I had a home, and friends, and I'd managed to fall in love. Even if he came with some serious baggage, I still loved him. With each thought of what I had, and not what I didn't have, I became myself again. The gravity of my thoughts didn't weigh me down.

"You have a choice. You are not a tree. You are not stuck. You always have a choice," I reprimanded myself, remembering that I could choose to let my depressing thoughts win, or I could get up. Focus on one heartbeat at a time. Get up.

"Get up," I told myself and rolled out of bed. My fingers twitched toward the sheets, to go back to the warm safe zone I'd created and lay there until darkness claimed me.

"Take a step." I shook my head and took a step, then another, then another.

"I need a shower."

If someone watched me fight against myself just to move and do simple things, I'm sure I'd be committed to the hospital again. It was hard to understand unless you'd been there, where simple acts of life were near impossible. Your body, your mind, and your soul tried to pull you so deep into hopelessness, that you could barely breathe.

I don't know what it is about a shower that brings out emotions, but the tears I'd held back since leaving the mansion descended. The spray of water blended with the salty tears of my pain being released, and my sobs stayed within the glass wall. My trembling body ached with every slick movement of the soap against my skin, but I didn't stop. I kept concentrating on doing the next step. Get clean, let the tears flow, then dry off.

Efforts to dress normally where tossing on a sweater, leggings, and boots became tiresome. I'd probably resembled a bridge troll more than a person but I had no one to impress right now. I had to eat and write down my jumbled thoughts. I became a journalist for the paper because I had a gift that could help. I loved writing, and I sought the truth. I'd become so good at my job that work didn't bother me, which in times like this I was grateful for.

Coffee warmed my hands as I made some oatmeal and sat at my table. Half of my notes were useless now. I knew who the killer was and knew his motives behind the murders. What I didn't know was what could be done about it. I couldn't have him arrested or use public outrage from the paper to take him down.

I was still on a dangerous deadline, with the people I cared about hanging in the balance.

"You cannot do this. You will fail," a voice whispered in my mind, like a snake hissing as it curled around me, suffocating me with the outcome of my failure.

"No!" I shouted. I closed my eyes. I couldn't listen to any voice that wanted me to give in. I wouldn't fail. There was no other option. I fail, I lose everyone, and the world will be run by the dead.

    I grabbed my notes on Rudy and began reading, looking for anything that would give me more insight into his mind and motives other than jealousy. From the research on him, I switched to my laptop and investigated ghost lore, consisting of articles people had published about the dead in the past, no matter how obtuse they might seem. I figured in all the years of history, the dead tried to rise before. One hour after another, I delved deeper into the next step, the next research until I found what I looked for and prepared for tomorrow, where I would fight against a curse for love.

Chapter Thirty-Three
Jude

"Quite the party happening out there. I cannot wait to mingle and soak up every bit of this night." Rudy shivered with barely contained excitement next to me, basking in my anger. He was dressed in a dapper suit, with an intricate devil's mask that stopped just above his nose.

"Don't look too sour, Jude. You're getting everything you wanted. To go out with a bang of a show, and I have a little surprise for you later." He patted me on the shoulder and I dreamed of breaking his fingers in half. I didn't care what he had planned, I would stop him before he got too far. After talking with the originator of the curse, I felt stronger and dived down deep into my power, stewing, waiting for the right time to unleash myself upon the dead.

"Let's just get this over with." I stepped into the ballroom where dozens of people gathered in ball gowns and masks. I imagined the scene before me matched the history of this mansion, when they used to have parties nearly every night. People danced, and they ate the food created in the magnificent kitchen by world-renowned chefs. Liquors and wines were used in toasts to the greatest party in Seahill's history. People celebrated life, and the mystery of Halloween.

"Happy Birthday, Jude Mallory!" the crowd shouted as I stood at the top of the stairs to the room, hating that so many people were here, and none of them cared for me or knew my story. They wanted fun and leisure with a show. The live orchestra that had been hired to play for the night silenced their instruments with a wave of my hand.

"Thank you all." I nodded at the people with a fake smile on my face, while my gaze searched for one person. Selene wasn't here yet, although she had been instructed to show by our unfortunate stringmaster, pulling us how he deemed fit toward fates we did not wish for.

"Thank you for coming to my home and lighting up the place. I hope you have enjoyed *Mystical* and will stay as long as you like on this haunted night. The show will start thirty minutes before midnight." I closed my welcome statement and walked down the stairs to mingle. My deathly power crept from my skin and wafted off me like smoke. It was Halloween, of course, so the people weren't bothered with death caressing them as I walked. It was easier this way, instead of keeping it bottled up.

The orchestra began playing again, and people danced and laughed carefree. I hoped Rudy hadn't poisoned the food so he could kill them and have more dead people at his disposal. The thought partially alarmed me, so I waved Joslyn over and asked her to please check it for me. She nodded and walked away with her tiger, everyone giving them a wide berth as they walked toward the buffet tables.

All the ghosts in the house were nearly alive. Only a faint blue shimmer could be seen signaling them as dead if you knew how to look. To a normal person, it looked like stage makeup had been applied to their bodies.

"You look nice, as always." Lucy walked over to me, wearing a short ball gown and a tight pink corset. Her hair was piled high on her head, and a pink lacy mask covered the skin around her shocking blue gaze that roamed down my black ringleader's suit, then back up to my hat.

"Thanks. You ready for tonight?" I asked softly. She nodded.

"Thank you." I don't think the two words would ever be enough, but they would have to do. Lucy was going to be putting herself on the line tonight for me and for this world. She was the only one who could do what needed to be done.

"He didn't do a shitty job getting this together. If it wasn't for the murders and lives at stake, I'd say he did a good job with the timeframe," Lucy said, while looking around at the crowd. Indeed

Rudy had put an insane amount of effort into this night, but it wasn't without cost.

"Excuse me. May I have the next dance?" a familiar voice called from behind me, and my heart picked up its pace. Lucy grinned, then walked away with a knowing look in her eyes.

"I'm not sure the love of my life would appreciate me dancing with another woman." I smirked, as I turned around slowly.

Selene was beautiful. She wore a Bohemian black dress with loose long sleeves and a slit that showed some of her creamy thigh. Desire slammed into my chest as the need to take her consumed me. Her hair was braided to the side and the black Venetian mask accentuated her look as a reaper. She was my deathly match in every way.

"I think she would make an exception for me. It is your birthday, after all." A sad smile graced her lips, and I forgot to breathe. My hands reached out and pulled her body close. She trembled in my arms, and her shoulder shook once. She wasn't OK. But she was here, and I knew how much strength she had to pull from the depths to show up and fake that all was OK.

"I love you." I didn't know if the words would ease her pain, but I wanted to say them. We only had this moment. Nothing beyond was guaranteed.

"I'm sorry," she whispered against my chest. My fingers lifted her chin gently, allowing me the honor to look into her eyes to see the emotions swirling in their depths.

"You have nothing to be sorry for. Now kiss me like you missed me, and let's dance." I smiled when she rolled her eyes but stood on her toes to reach my lips. Her kiss was like dying and living at the same time. She slowly pulled away and grabbed my free hand to hold out in a waltz position.

"I hope you know how to do this kind of dance because I have no clue," she admitted and I smiled again. I knew, since living in this house with ghosts who only knew how to dance the waltz had taught me the steps. Instead of telling her just how much experience I had in this department, I showed her.

I led her around the room, and she followed like we'd been doing this dance for centuries together. People stopped dancing as we passed by. The laughter and mutterings silenced and except for us, the rest of the room went dark. Nothing and no one existed in this moment but us, captivated in each other. The world simply melted away, along with the crowd, to give us space while we had our moment.

I may have been leading us in this dance, but I'd follow here wherever she went. I didn't care if that made me whipped, or a chained man. This woman held my heart and soul in her delicate hands, and I couldn't think of a better protector for it than her. When the orchestra ended the song and started another, we kept going. The lights grew brighter, and the crowd around us danced with laughter once more.

With Selene beside me, my confidence grew. Tonight would go as planned, and this nightmare would end without any lives being lost.

Another smile off to the side caught my attention and the warmth that had settled over me turned to ice. Rudy watched Selene and I dance with a smile on his face, too, only his expression hinted that everything was going according to *his* plan, which frightened me so much I wanted to steal Selene and run away right now.

But her friends in the Hero Society . . . I couldn't lose them, either.

It felt like a noose was already tightening around my neck, and all I could do was feel the squeeze on my life.

Chapter Thirty- Four
Selene

"Any news of where our friends are being held?" I managed to whisper to Jude, once we stopped dancing, and he walked us over toward the large buffet table.

"Not quite. He leaves the screen up with the video feed from that location. I don't believe it's far from here, and it looks like a warehouse of sorts." He leaned in close, his mouth against my neck as he spoke, so it seemed like he was nuzzling me instead of conversing about hostages. My hand reached up to his shoulder instinctively, fingers digging into his ringleader jacket.

"They are alive, though, I see them move a lot. Lilith talks to the ghosts and distracts them while the others talk." His words gave me hope. I still couldn't think about what would happen if we failed tonight.

"Do you have a plan?" I half-whispered, half-moaned as his lips caressed my skin, his tongue flicking the sensitive flesh.

"I do." He breathed and goosebumps rose on my skin.

"Me, too. Should we talk about it?" We needed to be a united front going against Rudy, but I doubted we'd get a chance to truly be alone. Even if a ghost was by us, listening, they wouldn't have heard anything they didn't already know.

"We can't." He confirmed what I had been thinking. Unease grew in my belly with the thought of two plans that could conflict or easily go wrong.

"Whoever's plan wins buys breakfast tomorrow?" Jude pulled back with a hopeful smile. I shook my head. I was about to reply with a smart-ass comment, when a tiger head nudged my free hand and Joslyn interrupted us.

"I need to borrow Selene. She'll be back for the show." She looked at Jude, and he must have seen something in her eyes that said she could be trusted. His hands released their grip on my body as he took a step back so I could follow the woman.

"I'll see you soon," he promised, and I nodded. The gnawing of unease grew into a knot that tightened my gut, and I knew . . . somehow I just knew . . . that when we saw each other again, there would not be emotions of joy.

Joslyn gripped my hand gingerly and led me away. I watched Jude for as long as I could without walking into anyone, afraid I wouldn't see him again.

"Don't fear, Selene, love always wins," Joslyn whispered to me, her voice so soft it seemed to carry with the music in the air.

Love always wins. A statement I needed to have faith in. It was something Phillip would say, especially when he knew what future was best. He couldn't offer those words to me now, but I could still have faith in a future where Jude and I were together. A future where my friends were safe and back to making the world a better place.

I'd seen the ghost that didn't belong here walking around, talking to other ghosts about what would happen after tonight. Rudy was going to break the gates to the afterlife according to the gossip between the wandering souls. I hoped it was only chatter and not laced with truth. We strolled up the stairs, then Joslyn stopped us before a door to a bedroom.

"You are safe in here and can speak freely." She looked down the hall to where a corpse with decomposed flesh hung from its bones like a shredded dog's toy. I opened the door to an immaculate room with a four-poster bed, hand-carved furniture, and a painting of a woman in a Victorian-style wedding dress standing next to a man in a suit. She looked so familiar, but I couldn't pinpoint where I'd seen her.

"It hasn't been that long since you've seen me. Surely you wouldn't have forgotten a face like mine." Madam Tully's voice chuckled near the window on the left of the painting. The knot in my stomach unraveled and instantly I released my tense posture.

"Thank you, Joslyn." The witch-ghost smiled at my guide, who closed the door as she turned to walk down the dimmed hall.

"We don't have a lot of time, but before anything else is discussed, I must tell you how proud I am of you." She floated over to me, her hands cradled my face tenderly.

"Thanks." I didn't know what she was proud of me for, but it was nice to hear.

"You rose without hope in your thoughts, against all odds, and are fighting for those you love. I could not have wished for a better match for my Jude than you, Selene." She hugged me, and even though my power urged me to take her onward, I gritted my teeth and embraced her.

"That boy has a wicked plan for you two. I've seen it, but if you keep that faith that's burning in your heart, you have a chance." She cupped my cheeks once more, then released me. She floated to the painting, her fingers caressing the canvas of her and her husband, Jude's great-great-grandfather.

"I wished I could have stopped him, but we can only control ourselves in the end. He was so consumed by the lavish life, a selfish life that he didn't give in to what nature demanded," she said remorsefully. The poor woman watched as her husband took a dark path that doomed everyone.

"I was young then. So caught up in the luxury and the parties. My coven pulled me away for a few weeks, trying to connect me back to my roots, and by the time I returned, it was too late. I've watched everyone I cared about die and remain in this limbo, drowning in pain.

"But that all changes tonight." She forced a smile on her lips, then twisted the knob of the closet beside her. She disappeared for a moment, then appeared again with a garment bag in her hands. She gently laid it on the bed, and I walked over, curiously.

"You need something borrowed, and it'll fit. We were the same size once upon a time." She winked and worked on opening the bag for me to see Madam Tully's wedding dress from the painting.

"Oh, no. He wouldn't." I wanted to weep from the notion that this dress would be needed. It was cruel for Rudy to make Jude and I marry tonight. I shook my head as sadness caught in my throat. Tears formed even as I tried to hold them back.

"He would, and he is. At the end of the show, Rudy will have you and Jude say your vows with a noose around Jude's neck." The grim line to her lips confirmed the truth. To think of this, to force this, only a monster would be so cruel.

But then a little voice inside my mind pushed past the dark hissing of failure and anger. I knew what I had to do. I found my ultimate truth, now that all the puzzle pieces in my head connected. The curse wasn't a promise to the ghosts that would break it but a promise made in death. One that binds a soul to another. Marriage!

"I'm gonna need help getting in this thing." With a smile on my lips, my fingers grasped onto the hanger of the dress.

"I never had a daughter to help get ready on her wedding day. I'd be honored to assist the future Mrs. Mallory." Madam Tully's devious smile solidified my thoughts, and now I knew what I had to do. She'd been telling us all along that we were the cure to our problem. It was inside us all along!

First, I needed to get ready for my wedding.

Chapter Thirty- Five
Jude

"Don't forget to meet me at the tower before the show ends." Rudy slapped me on the back in a brotherly gesture, which earned him a shrug from me.

"So sensitive. All right Mr. Ringleader. Do your stuff." He pointed toward the open area of the ballroom where I'd begin my last show. It felt bittersweet in a way. All I'd wanted before was this, to go out with a bang, but now all I wanted was Selene and her friends safe.

The crowd had been moved back, giving us enough space for the performances. I glanced at the large clock over the far wall to my right and remembered my orders. When there were five minutes remaining in the show, I was to head up to the tower, which could be seen from here and hang myself as the final act. Poetic, if the people below knew that it wasn't a magic trick and that I wouldn't be showing up somewhere else with a dove flying out of my hat.

My main performance partner, Rey the crow, flew onto my shoulder as I walked into the darkroom with a spotlight on my steps. He lived wild on the property but always came when he was needed. I'd rescued him when I was younger, and crows had a sense of justice that could never be forgotten. He used to leave me gifts by the door, so I'd leave it open for him every morning for a few hours. But he wasn't a house bird despite how amazing that would have been.

"What do you say, Rey? One last show?" I smiled and lifted my hand for him to step onto.

"Welcome to *Mystical's* final performance. Enjoy your last moments in this time as we surround your mind with the fantastical."

"Prepare to imagine." Rey spoke, a trick I never worked on with him. A part of me always thought he was a person trapped as a bird, but I could never prove my theory.

Lights came on from the chandeliers above, the opening to the tower revealed between them, and the performers were in full exhibition. The trapeze artist swung from the bars to the hanging crystal lights, then back to each other, flipping as they flew through the air. Lucy walked a tightrope while jumping up and back down, doing a cartwheel while the tiger pretended to lunge for her.

I raced around the room, disappearing with the help of Joslyn, and emerging onto the chandelier like we'd practiced. Without looking and without fear, I jumped. The wind from the wall rattled my clothes and skin, but then I wasn't falling anymore. I stood on the tightrope with Lucy holding my hand. Everyone was putting on the show of our lives, and I was sad it had to end.

With the clock nearing my final performance, I snuck from the room and walked up the creaky stairs toward the balcony of the tower. Every step closer to my death came with memories of how I had lived my life, the choices I'd made thinking I was doing the right thing at the time. I remembered when my mother and I made cookies before Christmas when I was five. We laughed and got flour everywhere. I pretended I was a ghost covered in the white baking ingredient with the dust following me around everywhere.

From childhood to adulthood, memories flashed through my head like a movie. As soon as I walked past the door to the balcony, I dropped to my knees from the cruel scene before me.

Tears fell onto the dust-covered wood with a splash. My hands instantly went to my lips in disbelief as Selene stood in front of me wearing Madam Tully's old wedding dress, looking like a Victorian princess with her hair piled on top her head. She was a vision from my deepest dream and horrifying nightmare at the same time.

"I thought you'd be happy, man. You get what you always wanted before the end." Rudy smiled from the corner of the space, and I had no fight to give him. Sobs ruined me in a way I'd never experienced before. Agony and bliss swirled inside me, fighting to be the dominating emotions.

I didn't know what to do or what to say.

"I don't wanna die." I shook my head, tears streaming down my cheeks as Selene collapsed to her knees before me. I didn't want to have her like this, only to leave her so soon. It wasn't enough time. I needed more time. I needed to turn back the clock to spend every hour of every day with her.

"Jude, I know this is a ploy designed by a hateful spirit to make you feel unimaginable pain. But I, Selene, want you for my husband. To love you and spend the rest of my days being your wife. Will you do me the honor of marrying me?" Her hands cradled my face. Her eyes shown bright with love in them. Love and hope. I shook my head but my words were the opposite of my movements.

"Yeah."

Her smile grew as she released my face to stand. Her hand stayed before me like a lifeline waiting to pull me from drowning. All I had to do was take her hand to enjoy the last bit of my life with her as mine. Even if that meant it was only for a few more minutes.

"How touching. Let's get this moving along so we can have our final deathly act, shall we?"

I glared at Rudy, promising agonizing pain, ghost or no. Somehow, someway, I would deal out justice for this.

My hand grasped onto Selene's, taking hold of the only feeling in the world that deserved my heart beating for. Love.

Madam Tully appeared next to a long rope with a noose tied at the end. I got where this was going and while I had my plan, I was also making peace with the fact that I would likely be dying no matter what tonight. Rudy had told me what he wanted from me in detail, and while I wanted to fight him, there were lives at stake. As if sensing my thoughts, he lifted a screen with the trapped Hero Society to prove a point.

"Your friends will die if you fight me, along with every innocent life in this mansion. You're out of options. Oh, and I wouldn't expect Lucy to help you with any of your plots to defeat me. I had her taken care of."

Of course he had. I knew she couldn't be injured because she was a ghost, but that didn't mean he couldn't detain her or make her part in our plan a struggle. Hopefully she would still be there to cut the rope as I fell to my death.

"Let's get this over with, shall we?" Madam Tully rolled her eyes at Rudy, then held her hands out for Selene and I to take.

"Jude, my sweet boy. Do you take Selene to be your wife in life and death? To help her rise when there is too much on her shoulders? To love her and cherish her?" Madam Tully smiled at me without sadness on her face.

"I do." I looked at my Selene while Rudy lifted the noose and tightened it around my neck.

"Selene, my brave girl. Do you take Jude to be your husband in life and death? To show him that life is worth living and not just existing in it? To love him and cherish him?"

Selene looked up at me with waiting tears of happiness for this moment. Despite what appeared to be an ending, this act was transformed into a beautiful beginning for us both.

"I do." Her words trembled slightly as the emotions she'd been holding were released.

"I love you, Jude, come what may."

"I love you, Selene, in life and death. My heart beats for you no matter what the coroner's say." I smiled at the sad attempt I'd given to make her laugh. It worked, and all I wanted was to kiss her just like that.

"I now bind you together in holy matrimony as husband and wife. You may kiss and seal the promise made on this sacred ground." Madam Tully clapped her hands together in prayer.

I distinctly heard the music begin to build. Every note brought my life closer and closer to the cue of death. Only I wasn't done living just yet. I had a wife to kiss.

Her hand reached up to touch my jaw, as my fingers laid over hers gently. Holding her touch against me if that's what it would take to stay with her like this forever. Our gaze never wavered as our lips were drawn to each other for this last gift.

Her lips were soft and tasted like tears and sweet cherry with every press against mine. My wife. My reason for living.

"Great. Enjoy hell, Jude."

Pain sliced into the hand holding Selene's as Rudy's strong hands pushed me away from her beckoning lips and I tumbled off the balcony toward a short fall and a snapped neck.

Chapter Thirty- Six
Selene

"Now!" I screamed and Trixie appeared behind Rudy with a murderous score to settle. He was her only unfinished business. When I asked for her help to take Rudy down, she came to the mansion with me and hid in the shadows until this moment. She wrapped her hands around him, trapping his spirit within her grip with the magical symbols we'd drawn on her shimmering skin. Now that he was contained for the moment, Madam Tully could work her spell that I'd found in the articles of my research from yesterday. Bind him from hurting anyone else until he could be dealt with.

There was no time to waste. Jude wouldn't have much time left if I didn't hurry. I had a plan, and even though it was crazy to leap after him and cut the rope, it was the only one I had.

Without thinking another thought, I gripped the small knife I'd hidden in my hand and trusted my crazy plan. On swift feet, I ran for the balcony's edge, then jumped off with my arms wide. Hands caught me with a jerk of my body slamming against the sudden hold on my hands. My focus shifted from the cut rope hanging from the tower above with no Jude attached to the face of Lilith who'd caught me before I could fall to my death.

"I've always wanted to do trapeze and swing from a chandelier with ghosts. Very exciting party." She giggled and released me into the air with a scream ripping from my lungs.

"I've got you, wife." Jude's grip latched onto me as he swung upside down with only his legs holding him on the trapeze bar. It appeared that his plan had worked, since he wasn't hanging from the rope. Instead, I wished we had a moment earlier to discuss everything before we tried to do the same thing a different way. Jude looked around and then shifted his gaze back to me.

"Jude, we need to get to the gates, like now," I urged him and he nodded.

"Trust me, OK? I need you to turn reaper now." He paused and I nodded. Seconds later we fell with terrified screams from the crowd watching us plummet to the polished marble floors below. I closed my eyes without hesitation, my hands in Jude's as I became one with my powers. A lightness lifted my soul as I separated from my body into that realm of the afterlife. Yet, I still felt Jude with me, tethering me between two worlds. I vaguely felt my physical form being caught by someone, which was a relief that I wouldn't be stuck as a soul after today.

I opened my eyes as an arm wrapped around Jude and he turned a shimmering blue color.

"No!" He could not become a ghost. I wouldn't take him onward. That would be the end of me.

"Trust me," he whispered as our scenery turned black, then light, then dark, then we landed in a room I'd hoped I would never see again.

"Go, Lucy. Get out of here." Jude pushed his ghostly friend away from the gates to the afterlife that called to her with sweet words of peace.

It took a few seconds for me to catch up, but once I realized she had helped Jude and me float through the house like ghosts do, we were now in a room that threatened her soul. She did this for Jude, for us, and for everyone up there.

She took a step with an outreached hand toward the gates. Disappearing tears flew past her as a burst of wind pushed Jude and me back from the gates.

We did everything that was needed to seal the broken part where the souls had been able to slip out. Now the only part of the curse left was the blood paid. Our blood.

"We need to touch the gates together!" I yelled at Jude as the voices in my head tried to tell me to give up and accept my hopeless life. Only I knew those voices were lies, and I wouldn't give up. This awful room wanted me to fail, to walk into the afterlife like they had the first time Jude had shown it to me.

"After you, wife." Jude held his still bleeding hand toward my matching one. I'd felt a hint of remorse for cutting his hand before, but I didn't know if I'd get another chance to do so. Part of me had hoped that just droplets of his blood on the ground mixed with mine would do the deed, but that wasn't the case. I gripped him, our blood mingling together, truly binding us in this life and the next. No matter what happened in this life, we'd find each other in the next.

We walked together, past a stalled Lucy who was torn between choices for her to follow in her head. She could walk to the gates and burn or run. It seemed like a simple choice but those blasphemous gates were like sirens luring her to her true death.

"One, two . . ." Jude counted and together we pressed our bleeding hands against the gates.

Pain, sorrow, and joy filled my blood as the gates sucked power from me. Exhausted, I could barely stand.

"Love always wins, right?" I laughed with a shaky voice toward Jude and he gave me no answer.

A bright light blinded me, filling my soul with peace and love. One minute we were in a frightful nightmare with a curse and the gates to the afterlife. Then the next moment we lay on the ballroom floor, confused as to what happened and where we landed.

"What the—?" I blinked over and over, hoping to understand what my eyes saw. Dorian stood before me with my physical body in his arms.

"I caught you." I swooned from his words and relief sagged against my chest. I closed my eyes and went back into one of both spirit and body. I'd never used my gifts like I had tonight, so I felt woozy as Dorian lowered my legs to the ground.

"You're all here. You made it." I smiled at all of my friends.

"What is super speed and changing into an animal against ghosts? Not shit. But put an empath and a boy genius in the room with one and you have one hell of an escape and therapy session." Phillip's arms wrapped around me with a shit-eating grin on his face. I wanted to smack him on the arm for this whole thing. Of course he knew all of this would happen.

"It could have gone many different ways, but I gambled on love, and love always wins." He released his hold and winked. He had bet that Jude and I would fall in love and break the curse.

"Glad everyone is all right. Now I've got a bunch of dead to send to the afterlife. I'll talk later." Jude had interrupted, the deathly darkness billowing from his body in waves toward every ghost in the room. The crowd that was still watching us like this was part of the show cheered, while some gasped when they realized this wasn't a trick.

My power hummed alongside his. He was my match calling me to join in this feast of death. This I could do.

Angry ghosts who Rudy had convinced to join his team rushed us with weapons but Jude's power wrapped around their throats.

"If you would do the honors, wife." I nodded. There were at least ten ghosts within Jude's hold. And while I knew he could send them away to the afterlife himself, he was letting me have a little fun . . . payback for what had been done the past few days.

Every soul I touched became black and red. A horrible aura of hell grabbed them before they disappeared. Not one of the ten carried a heart of light to find peace beyond this life. A shame, but they had made their choices.

"Oh shit," Asher cursed as he looked around the room and muttered beneath his breath. One by one, the people in the crowd collapsed to the ground.

"Did you kill them?" Echo cursed at her soul mate, running over to check on a masked woman's neck for a pulse.

"No, but I put them to sleep. There is a horrid darkness on the ground outside and they did not need to witness what's to come."

We all ran to the back of the house to look upon the cemetery down the hill. Emily reached my side and squeezed my hand gently. I wished she hadn't been involved with this mess, but her spirit calmed me. We turned as the sound of footsteps echoed on the porch behind us.

"So it begins . . . the heroes against the dead, now that love has conquered the curse." Madam Tully arrived, with her hands lifted toward the sky just as lightning crashed throughout the darkness. Hundreds of torches lit throughout the graveyard, illuminating the small army of corpses that crept up the hill.

Chapter Thirty- Seven
Jude

I knew Rudy had been planning a stunt like this. Half of me expected him to ride on a skeleton horse in front of his army like a dead general. My family—the ghosts who had been trapped at Mallory Mansion—hid behind or within their tombs as the corpses limped toward us like a scene from a zombie movie.

"We can hurt those kinds of dead people, right?" Rose asked with a slight tremor of her lips, and I replied with the only answer I knew.

"We can try."

Selene's hand wrapped in mine and squeezed once before letting go. She eyed the army with defiance. It was too early to think about what had happened minutes ago in the cursed room of the gates. Though I sensed the change within me—a cleaned and forged power within my veins—I refused to accept them. Later, when this whole night ended and I woke up in the morning with Selene in my arms would I accept that it was truly over.

"Let's go kick some dead ass!!" Lilith hooted and was the first to start running to meet the army ahead of us. Her lover, Leon, raced after her with super speed and was the first to punch a corpse back twenty yards.

I didn't feel back for them, they were dead anyways and chose to escape from the afterlife and follow a blind with hatred ghost. They deserved to be taken back to hell with an ass beating.

Soon everyone had a corpse descend on them with hands outstretched and mouths wide to attack. Some were quick, and some were slow. I snarled as two rotting men tried to grasp my neck, ready to twist, but my power gripped them and ripped them in two.

"They aren't dying!" someone shouted as I saw the torn pieces of a decomposing man still moving. It wouldn't be as easy to destroy bodies as it was to release the souls.

"You have to open the gates and take them back. It's your job to protect mankind from the dead," Selene called out from my right as she touched a corpse and its soul combusted into a variety of red and golds. It would take a lot of power out of me, but she was right. I had to go back to the gates and use them properly. My fight wasn't out here with the rest of my friends. It was inside the mansion.

My great-great-grandfather had shared with me his pain of being the one to bring the curse upon the Mallory family. He'd spent his whole afterlife hiding at the dark mausoleum as penance for the sorrow he had brought upon those he cared about. He had told me how to open the gates, and how to close them, something he'd never shared with any of his descendants before me. None of them ever bothered to talk to him, to utter the words he'd been dreaming of for so long. Words about forgiveness. In the end of our talk. He believed I was the true heir of the Hades power. That it may have let each of the Mallory men in the family take a turn but would only yield to me. The crazy thing was I believed him. I left him at the crypt with the hope he'd forgive himself as I had forgiven him, and join us at the mansion, maybe even see his wife who stood watching us all battle against corpses.

"Dorian!" I howled at the demigod, and he flashed toward me while keeping an eye on Esme.

"I need you to take me to a room in my house. You teleport, right? It's how you got them all here from wherever you were taken hostage?"

The man nodded and grabbed my shoulder. I hadn't told him exactly where to go, but he knew. The room was empty and remorse flooded through me with the thought of Lucy having been too close to the gates to fight off the draw toward the other side, her soul's death. But now wasn't the time. I'd search for her later.

My tendrils of power curved around each golden rod of the gates, twisting and pulling until the gold was no longer seen beyond the black death that covered every inch.

"I am the keeper of the gates, and the master of death. By my right, bestowed upon me by Hades, you will open." My great-great-grandfather had made me practice the words at least a dozen times before I had left his crypt.

With a creaking shudder, the gates did as they were told. Peace called to me, and somehow, I knew I could go into the sweet heaven that coddled me. But my heaven wasn't in there, it was above me, fighting the dead beside her friends. Fighting for mankind.

With the gates open, I roared with every strength I had left and released my power through the mansion in search of evil souls that needed to be returned from the hell in which they had come. One by one, my power tangled around a soul and dragged them past the gates. I'd never used my gifts this extensively, and while I was exhausted, I shed my chains, and became free. Like my power had been born for this moment, waiting to be unleashed at this magnitude.

Souls from corpses fighting the Hero Society were ripped from their composing flesh and screamed as they disappeared beyond my sight into the red-and-gold haze behind the gates. When the last of my power returned with a soul of hate and jealousy weaved within its very core, I smiled.

"I'm taking him on, my right as one of his victims, but you can rough him up before I do." Trixie stood beside a broken Rudy, whose pleading eyes begged for mercy. For once I was glad Selene wasn't by my side since we had become husband and wife. She didn't need to see what I intended to do to my old friend. He'd killed innocent women just to fuck with me, and he'd nearly killed me. Threatened our friends and rose an army of the dead to take over the world one city at a time. But most of all, he had tried to take Selene away from me, and I could not forgive him.

"You might wanna close your eyes," I warned Trixie, but she stood steadfast.

"No, I think I'll watch."

Most heroes wouldn't harm another human. But Rudy was already dead, so technically I couldn't actually hurt him. However, I could make him feel everything like he was really alive.

Maybe I was more of an anti-hero, with a good conscience capable of being bad if the right justice demanded it. Rudy would be given judgment once he walked past those gates and that would be decided from the stains on his soul. I wouldn't be the one to deliver that on him. He'd face his maker on his own.

A caw echoed around the room and suddenly Rey landed on my shoulder. He had impeccable timing as usual. He had to have some sort of magic beneath his feathers. Crows never forgot a face, especially a face who had wronged them. Rey loved me. He was here for justice, too.

Rey made the first move, then my power dug into Rudy's flesh. Rudy's pain-filled screams fell on ears that relished in his suffering. Two wrongs didn't make a right, but they did make me feel like I could sleep better after this. Trixie would find peace once she brought him to the afterlife herself.

I'd have the rest of my life attempting to repent for the wrongdoings that occurred in front of the gates.

Chapter Thirty- Eight
Selene

The battle ended and boy was it a stinky way to conclude the night.

The souls within the corpses were dragged to the gates via Jude's immense power, but their bodies stayed behind. I didn't want to think about what needed to be done with the piles of rotting flesh strewn over the grass.

"Now that they aren't trying to kill us, I think I may throw up." Esme covered her lips while her face turned green. She moved swiftly toward the mansion without another word.

"I motion we head back inside where that strange light is coming from." Lilith pointed toward the mansion, where indeed a bright light beamed from the roof into the clouds. My powers stirred, and a sweet inner peace surround me like when I was near the afterlife that resembled heaven.

"Oh! We're free! We can finally leave!" The four hitchhiking ghosts hauled ass toward the light, and soon there was an exodus of ghosts heading toward the open gates that would lead them to their peaceful afterlife.

I'm sure some souls would choose to stay here, but many were tired of being trapped. They wasted no time, and no goodbyes heading onward.

One by one, we entered the mansion to the ballroom where the crowd laying on the floor slept blissfully unaware of everything that happened around them. Performers from Jude's circus surrounded a lone man who stood in front of the bright light with a confidence only a ringleader could have.

"We'll never forget you." The trapeze artists walked into the bright beam after waving to him, then floated up like the light was an elevator to heaven. Many ghosts stopped to talk to Jude before they left this Earth, in which he'd embrace them, then urge them to be free of this place.

Joslyn and her tiger and the little boy and his pet elephant walked together into the light with big smiles. The sight was beautiful, and even though I assumed I had no more tears to cry, little tears fell while I watched these souls find peace.

"Never seen a sight like this before," Draco murmured in awe. I looked at my friends, who were enraptured by the scene before them. It wasn't every day you saw the dead rise and the dead find peace, wherever that was to them. There were still some ghosts in the house, standing to the side without the desire to move onward. They watched their friends go with happy expressions, waving goodbye. Their time to go would come, but they had unfinished business they wanted to complete. I understood, so I kept my power away from them.

One last figure walked toward Jude. The only soul left who wished to leave. Lucy.

Despite everything she'd said before this night, Lucy risked her soul for us.

"Thank you for trusting me." She spoke to Jude but then turned her head toward me as well. She meant her words for the both of us.

"Thank you for saving us." I drifted from the Hero Society group and walked toward the single ghost and Jude. Jude's power pulsed in response to my movements. Oh boy. This was going to be an interesting wedding night.

"I wish you guys a happy marriage. Maybe you should name your firstborn Lucy." She winked and gently touched Jude on the shoulder before giving me a knowing look. With a performer's flair, she twisted her body into a flip and landed perfectly for a tightrope act into the light.

We watched her disappear, then Jude bellowed words for the gates to close. It took only seconds, and the light disappeared, too.

"My wife," Jude growled as his hands gripped my shoulders, pulling me toward his hard, warm-blooded body with a heart that thumped beneath his chest.

"Husband," I teased innocently, which brought about my favorite smirk on his face.

"I think your plan won tonight." He tucked me into his side as our friends came closer, wanting to get in on the hugs and celebrations.

"Now that we've saved mankind and they have no clue, again, I think I'll wake them up and we end this party." Asher slapped his hands together, ready to work his wild magic.

"I hope tonight ends with sleep."

"I vote it ends with a cup of tea."

"We're having sex tonight."

Of course Lilith made everyone laugh as the crowd began to rise, unaware of what had just happened around them. The smell outside the mansion would probably chase them back to their cars quickly, but besides that, they had no clue we'd just battled an army of the dead.

"I think I'm gonna celebrate November first with my wife. Everyone can see themselves out," Jude announced loud enough so the crowd heard. People grumbled about being suddenly exhausted and walked toward the exit.

"I think we're gonna head out, too." Esme peered at Dorian, who watched the crowd leave in all their finery.

"Us, too." Rose hugged Draco tightly, then they waved us goodbye and departed.

All our friends were safe. My husband swept me off my feet and walked swiftly toward his room.

"Happy November first, you two." Madam Tully bid us a goodnight as she walked with her arm tucked into a man down the hall. I vaguely wondered who the man was since he looked familiar to me, even in ghost form.

"That would be my great-great-grandfather." Jude answered my thoughts, as he took the stairs two at a time. He opened the door to his room with ease and set me down onto my toes after crossing the threshold as husband and wife.

I wanted to take my time with him and revel that this man was mine. I'd get to keep him. However, I knew that just because he wasn't destined to die on his thirtieth birthday anymore didn't mean he wouldn't die one day.

My hands ripped at his jacket and the button of his slacks.

"In a hurry?" he teased, but his eager fingers were at the pearl buttons of my old dress with haste, as well.

"Well you know, tomorrow isn't guaranteed, especially if you snore tonight." The dress dropped from my shoulders and puddled on the floor.

"Happy late birthday, Jude." His gaze devoured my bare skin as I stepped away from my dress and lifted onto my toes, our lips a breath away from each other.

"And here's to many more with you." I meant to gently press my lips against his, but he had other plans that quickly moved us to the bed.

We'd found our heaven in this life and vowed to live each heartbeat like it was our last, to thrive in the light with love, then exist in the darkness without each other.

"I think my birthday is going to be my favorite day of the year," Jude moaned, as he settled between my legs. His hand reached up to take off the last bit of clothing he had forgotten.

"Keep the hat on." I stopped his hand, and then Jude Mallory, the mysterious ringleader who lived in a haunted mansion, made love to his wife.

Epilogue
Three Hundred and Sixty-Four days Later
Jude

"Happy birthday to youuuu!" The group around me sang, and for the second birthday in a row, I had something to smile about. I'd gotten to live beyond my thirtieth birthday, which made me the oldest Mallory in over a century.

"Make a wish, you old man!" Asher hooted and I made a mental note to give him shit later about his dig. In the past year, I'd moved in with Selene and became friends with the Hero Society who stood next to me against the dead one year ago. The boys accepted me without hesitation, and while my power wasn't much help against the living, I still tried to assist as much as I could.

I'd turned the mansion into a museum. The Seahill Association of History had been beside themselves when I proposed the idea, and people came from all around the world to look at Mallory Mansion. We'd cleaned it up, restoring the beauty in the intricate details, and turned what was once a haunted home into a top destination for weddings and ghost hunters.

"I already have everything I could wish for," I laughed to my friends as a soft hand rested on my shoulder. Instinctively, my fingers grasped onto the hand in comfort, remembering all we went through to get to this moment. Selene and I had relished every second since our wedding night.

"Just hurry up, blow out your candles, and make a wish. I want a slice of that cake." Draco rarely voiced his sense of humor, but with his little one growing within the safety of Rose's belly, he had something to bring out the true joy in the everyday moments. He couldn't stop himself from laughing and teasing the other members of the crew.

Gwendolyn's robot friends jumped on the cake and waited patiently. It was unnerving at first to see robots act like they were real but after having dealt with a life of ghosts, I got over the reaction quickly.

"How about for a little girl?" Selene whispered in my ear, so softly I didn't think anyone else in the room heard her.

The candles were forgotten for a moment as I turned to face my wife. We hadn't exactly been trying for a baby, but I'd shared with her months ago that having a baby had been another one of my secret dreams besides getting married.

"You're serious?"

She nodded, her bottom lip pulled between her teeth nervously.

Without a word, I turned and blew out my candles on the large, homemade cake . . . my first birthday cake in decades.

I wished for many more birthdays to come with my family and friends. I wasn't going to part from this world easily, when I had them around. Now with a baby on the way, I made a promise to the universe that I would do anything to keep that babe safe, to love the baby and its mother as long as my heart beat in this world, then into the afterlife.

"I'm gonna be a father!" I hollered to the group of people who cared for us, and I wrapped Selene in the safety of my arms. My fingers drifted over her still small belly that would swell with the product of our love.

Now I had one more reason to love my birthday—the day I was supposed to die. Instead, I started a new life where I didn't just exist. I lived.

The End

Sneak Peek of Spring

His blue eyes stared at me so intensely, I sensed the need to move from where I sat on the couch, watching the newest episode of my favorite show. It was rare for me to be able to sit down and watch one of my shows not on the DVR, and he was ruining my mood by being surly and stoic.

"I doubt anyone is going to attack me while I sit in my living room wearing my sweater. No one's hiding beneath the couch, so can you go outside the room or something. Your stare is annoying."

His stare wasn't really annoying . . . it was annoying that the young, fifteen-year-old Hazel inside my heart, had been in love with him and had liked his eyes upon me, even if it was only for my protection. But Maddox had been gone a long time from my life, and now we were two different people: a hippie singer and a Green Beret. My temporary bodyguard who I didn't need.

I'd hoped he left, but instead he remained at his chosen post. Fine, if he wanted to be a pain in the ass, then I would be one right back. I stretched toward the sky, then took off my oversized sweater. A body was a body to me, and I embraced my own beauty long ago. However, being close to a naked person freaked many people out, and right now I was willing to use my body as a tool to make him feel uncomfortable.

Sitting back on the couch in nothing but my nakedness, I reached over to the coffee table and grabbed my teacup with a big smile on my face. Sucker. Barely paying attention to the show, I listened for his large frame moving to the door.

But it never came.

The man was impossible! The whole situation was ridiculous. I was perfectly capable of handling myself against anyone who tried to hurt me. I was part of the Hero Society and had eighty-three saves on my hero belt. Of course, I couldn't tell my label that. To them I was Hazel James, five-time platinum-record singer and advocate hippie for all green life. Plants and trees were my jam. However, what they didn't know was that at night, I was someone else. In my hero suit, I became a warrior, using my power over plants to help save lives and protect the innocent.

Maddox was completely unnecessary. There was no need for his massive body to be so close all the time or his blond hair and beard to smell like a crisp breeze from the frosty mountains. There was no need for him to look at me with those same eyes that I'd once written songs about in my teenage bedroom.

I had to get rid of him somehow. Suddenly, an idea occurred to me, guaranteed to get Maddox out of my life as easily as he had before.

Eat your heart out, Maddox Kennedy, you have no idea who you just agreed to bodyguard. I wasn't the Hazel he remembered, and it was time I introduced him to the new and improved Hazel.

Spring (Hero Society #7)
Standalone

Summer (Hero Society #8)
Standalone

~Original Hero Society series~

Dawn (Hero Society #1)

Day (Hero Society #2)

Dusk (Hero Society #3)

Night (Hero Society #4)

More Books by Jessica Florence

https://www.jessicaflorenceauthor.com/books

To stay up to date on all things Jessica Florence, including sales, releases, and a choose your own adventure story. Sign up for my Newsletter!!!

Dawn (Hero Society #1)

Dawn has come, a time for heroes to rise. Draco has lived long and felt the pain of loss more than anyone in one lifetime could imagine.

Immortality was given to him as a gift, a gift that failed him and turned him into a shell of the man that has nothing left but to wait out the end of existence alone.

Until her.

Rose is an empath who sees more than who Draco is supposed to be: she sees him, and what they could be. Together, they will begin the search for others with extraordinary powers, to stop a war that's been brewing for over a millennia.

The journey is only beginning, and an unnamed enemy has started to make his mark on their world.

The dawn of heroes has finally arrived.

Only time will tell if it's too late to defeat the upcoming darkness of night that now descends upon all of mankind.

The Final KO

I fight for a living.

Which makes finding a decent guy hard when you're a female MMA fighter. None of them have been my equal. I yearn for a man who can push me to reach new heights and challenge me. A man who will treat me like a lady then lift me up by my ass and impale me against the wall.

But when Arson Kade, MMA's top fighter and notorious manwhore, declares he's that man for me I have my doubts. Any sane woman would.

There seems to be more to Arson than the rumors that surround him, but will it make me fall hard or run for the hills?
I know I've got no choice but to hold on for the ride.

It's the main event and my heart's on the line.
But will it be the Final KO?

The Final Chase

I never thought one day I'd make a bet about pedicures to a man and loose.

But of course, I'd never man like him.
Jake Wild. Owner of Wild rescue for exotic animals.
He's everything I'm not, my polar opposite.
I'm heels and my salon,
He's dirt and his creatures.
But much like the animals he cares for, he's got that carnal edge.
He's the type of man you crawl on your hands and knees for.
He bites, he's on the hunt, and now I'm his prey
A chance meeting and a bet started the undeniable attraction between us.
But I'm not giving my heart and soul away that easy, he's going to have to catch me first.
It's the ultimate game of cat and mouse,
But will it be our Final Chase?

Long Drive

There is a long road in everyone's journey in life.
For some people, it's a way to get from one place to another.
For others, it's a search for one's purpose in existence.
For me, the road was where I could find peace.
When everything in my life had shattered, I turned to the road.
And that's where I met him.
Killian Lemarque.
A beautiful truck driver, and my salvation.
One month on the road together is the deal, and when it's over, I will have hopefully figured out what I'm going to do about my torn reality.
But sometimes the road can change everything.
Falling in love wasn't part of my plan nor his.

But here we are.
One Month. One Truck. One Long Drive.

How You Get The Girl

As Hollywood's hottest actor, getting a woman in my bed is never a challenge.

But after seeing a feisty woman in bar who was looking for a one-night stand, I knew that her being in my bed wouldn't be enough.

She turned me down, and I thought I'd never see her again.

Fate had other plans though.

Alessandra Rose is now my lead makeup artist for the next four months. Literally, her job is to touch me every day for the duration of filming. Sounds like a win, right?

Nope, she stops me at every hint of a flirt. I'm in uncharted waters for once.

Her argument is good I'll give her that. I'm a good actor, so accepting that it's not all an act would be tough.

But I'm not going anywhere; here heart is my Grammy and him here to win it.

That's how you get the girl

INSPIRED

Call it pure desperation, or maybe we'd agree it was the lack of sleep that had me signing six weeks of my life away to be bossed around by a life coach. Either way, I was trying to get my life together, and Logan Woodland was going to help.

I thought he'd make me eat healthier, drink more water, and do yoga. What I wasn't expecting, was to be forced to see myself as I was and how far I'd fallen.

But then his program worked.

He'd shown me a life filled with passion and desire. A life where I was stronger and could be the woman I'd never known existed inside me.

I did have a six-week life-changing experience, but now, I wanted more than I'd signed on for.

Him.

Guiding Lights

He sings of suffering. His eyes hold the pain of living in sorrow.
The moment our gaze meets recognition flares within.
We are tortured souls drifting in a sea of darkness.
He knows I have secrets that I'll never tell.
I am numb.
I am broken.
I can never be the guiding light through the darkness he thinks I am.
I have forsaken my past, I rely on keeping myself shut off.
I wish things were different, that maybe we could be each other's lifeline.
But destiny drags us down like an anchor.
He lives his life in the lime light of a famous rock star, and I live in shadows on the run.

I wished I'd known that before I fell for him, but now it's too late.

Blinding Lights

She dances with a passion I'll never know.
Seeing her again tears me at the seams.
She was never mine.
My soul is stained with the darkness of death.
I have killed.
I have tortured.
I have lost.
Her soul is too bright for the shadows I live in
and her determination to be the flame in my heart
could kill us both.
Still, I want her, I crave her.
But not even her blinding lights can fight away the
darkness threatening us both.

But I refuse to lose her, and this time I don't think I
can walk away.

Weighing of the Heart

What happens when the myths of old become reality?

Thalia Alexander has lived her life in peace until her twenty-fifth birthday when she has a strange dream about a man.

A tall, dark, and sexy man that shows up at her work the next morning.

Tristan Jacks is trouble with a capital T, but for some strange reason she is drawn to him like nothing she has ever experienced before. He has this possessiveness and adoration for her that she can't explain. It's like they have known each other forever.

Thalia's strange dreams continue to stalk her as her relationship with Tristan builds to be a love that will last the ages.

And when those dreams and reality start to clash, will Thalia be able to handle the truth?

Could the world of ancient myths truly exist in modern times?

Evergreen

It was supposed to be an easy stakeout.
Until a bunch of bachelorettes mobbed me, changing my life forever.

I couldn't get Andi Slaton, with her red hair, blue eyes, and cotton candy-flavored lip gloss, out of my head.

But when she offers herself to aid the FBI to help me take down the biggest criminal family in Tampa, Florida, my very sanity is put to the test watching her spend time with my arch enemy.

She's everything I want, I will be everything to her. We will be Evergreen.

Playlist

The Greatest Show- The Greatest Showman Cast

Rewrite The Stars- The Greatest Showman Cast

Night Falls- Descendants 3 Cast

You're Going Down- Sick Puppies

When World's Collide- Powerman 5000

Underneath- Cobi

Jungle- Jamie N Commons & X Ambassadors

Follow You Into The Dark- Death Cab For Cutie

The Next Right Thing- Kristen Bell

You Are The Reason- Callum Scott

Acknowledgments

I can't believe this is my 19th book written. Can I just thank you for reading it, for picking up this book?

Readers, you guys are my life. I will never get tired of saying how thankful I am for you. For your support whether you are new to my stories or a seasoned fan. I am honored, so honored to be a part of your life.

My Alpha readers, girls, I don't know what I'd do without you helping through my books. Autumn, Melissa, Krystal, Tina, Laura, I love you girls.

Dearest Bloggers and Bookstagrammers, I know I say it a lot but I literally couldn't do this without you!! No one would see about my book without you, period! I am so grateful to have you on my team.

Sarah, my goddess divine, the Hero Society wouldn't be the HERO SOCIETY without you. You make them real with your epic covers!

Lorraine, I don't know how I survived writing all my previous books without you. My craft has grown and I have become a better writer because of you. Thank youuu!

Virginia, your proofreading skills are the cherry on top of my book. I am so thankful to work with you! Always so kind, and accommodating!

Graceley, Amelia, K. Webster, Kate.. You ladies keep me together when I feel like I'm falling apart. Thank you for being amazing friends.

To my peanut butter baby, I love you so much you stinker.

And finally, to my husband. Thank you for supporting me, it means so much that you let me write and just get it. I am honored to be your wife, and to have you in my life with me. I don't think I could write such romantic books if I didn't have you.

<3

About the Author

Jessica Florence writes the stories that her fellow nerds yearn for.

From Superheroes to Sexy Truckers, Jessica is known to give readers unique tales of hope where love conquers all. Stories that melt away reality and take you on a journey with the characters. If escapism is what you are looking for, then look no further. Jessica is the Queen of weaving the tales you may not normally pick up but find yourself not being able to put down.

Jessica's always had a love of reading, and her love of books lead her to start writing in the 9th grade. She quickly learned that storytelling was her passion. Inspired by movies, music, and her personal life she writes like it's the very air she breathes. Through her writing it's evident that she lives for the stories she creates.

Jessica grew up in North Carolina, and currently resides in Southwest Florida with her daughter, husband, and German Shepherd. She loves to be outside, write in her hammock, and collect tea mugs.

CONNECT WITH J-FLO:

→ FACEBOOK:

facebook.com/jessicaflorenceauthor
→ INSTAGRAM:
Instagram.com/authorjessicaflorence
→ TWITTER: twitter.com/@Florence_jess
→ PINTEREST: pinterest.com/florencejess
→ WEBSITE: www.Jessicaflorenceauthor.com

Printed in Great Britain
by Amazon